THE FIFTH PRINCIPLE

July, 18, 2019

For Molly,
It's not "light" but
lightness is not the
nature of our work
as therapists.
I've so enjoyed
working with you & hope
it continues. And I
wanted to mark
(outwardly) this
transition.
with much
warmth,
Abby

The Fifth Principle

Paul Williams

KARNAC

First published 2010 by
Karnac Books Ltd.
118 Finchley Road
London NW3 5HT

British Library Cataloguing in Publication Data
A C.I.P. is available for this book from the British
Library.

ISBN-13: 978-1-85575-789-9

www.karnacbooks.com

For Carole and Patricia
In memory of Maureen and Ivor

How to kill a living thing

Neglect it
Criticise it to its face
Say how it kills the light
Traps all the rubbish
Bores you with its green

Continually
Harden your heart
Then
Cut it down close
To the root as possible

Forget it
For a week or a month
Return with an axe
Split it with one blow
Insert a stone

To keep the wound wide open

> —*Eibhlin Nic Eochaidh.* In: *Staying Alive: Real
> Poems for Unreal Times* (Bloodaxe, 2002).

Never again will you be capable of ordinary human
feeling. Everything will be dead inside you. Never
again will you be capable of love, or friendship, or
joy of living, or laughter, or curiosity, or courage, or
integrity. You will be hollow. We shall squeeze you
empty, and then we shall fill you with ourselves.

> —George Orwell, *1984*

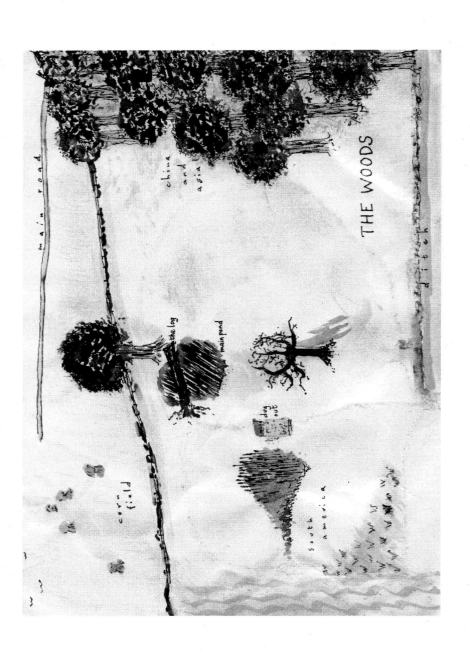

CONTENTS

PREFACE

This book is the first of three that take as their subject aspects of the author's life. The book reflects upon a period between birth and eight years of age; the second book will address adolescence and the third, adulthood.

It would be misleading to consider what follows to be autobiography, or the "case history" of an individual. The author of the book, and the individual written about, are not the same person. It is a piece of literature that furnishes an account of the methods of a mind in its efforts to prevail in oppressive circumstances. The author has undertaken, on behalf of the subject, to provide a faithful, intelligible rendering of unintelligible events. The mind in question, insofar as it resembles other minds, will speak to the reader in ways that are recognisable, though some of the things that are written about may be unfamiliar. The extent to which the account finds a home in the mind and imagination of the reader will be the measure of its worth.

Paul Williams
Oileáin Árainn
Eire
2009

MEMORIES

How do you know which of your memories is the first? Mine seem to fluctuate, so I am never quite sure which, if any, is the earliest. Sometimes I can recall looking up at clouds, transfixed and alarmed by the vast, random movements. At other times, I remember feeling cold and still. I think I am lying in a pram, staring at what must be the sun, at dusk, slipping out of a darkening sky. "Just wait. If you wait, you will be carried into the gold," a comforting voice says.

At other times, I can feel detached, drifting silently in space with no awareness of my body, and with a mind that seems to have seized, perhaps out of fear, although I don't feel this. I am numb.

"There is nothing to do, nowhere to go," is the refrain. I can't say if this memory was an event, whether it came later, or who, if anyone, said it or anything like it. Occasionally, I glimpse a boy (these days it might be my son) slip and fall to his death. I have rarely fallen asleep without a version of this picture and each time, as with most of these thoughts and memories, there is a foreboding and unexpected shock that no amount of familiarity or preparation can ward off. I find myself rudderless, imperceptibly small and taken to a place where all that is inside me seems to be emptied out, whilst nearby, something appalling is taking place. This emptying out may have come to define me. It became more familiar to me than any other state of mind I know. Insubstantial, without redemption and filled with dread, I became alien, on the verge of disappearing, unable to think, speak or help myself.

I can't sleep. In fact, I have never been able to sleep and have never understood why. It's not that I can't fall asleep, but more that I remain awake whilst asleep, watching, waiting, without a capacity to rest. This has been so for as long as I can remember. Waiting for what? What is so important that I must not sleep? Does it have anything to do with why other people can't sleep? Are we so afraid that each filament must guard against life itself? If so, why? When we are sleep, we usher in a life that is more truthful and more disturbing than anything we have ever said or done. Is this life more authentic, or is it something diabolical that presses on us so hard that the prospect of sleep becomes terrifying? For those who cannot sleep, the prospect of death may come to feel like sweet reason, akin to a concerned parent ministering to a sick child. Perhaps many more of us than we realise edge ourselves towards a death that we understand very well, as we have prepared for it so often in life on the basis of a tacit promise that we will become calmer, less afraid, like babies who let go and slip into a dreamless dream, from a time before time began, a dream unlike any other, a dream of perpetual peace.

Why do I think these things, when I know they bring torment? Not just to me, but to anyone who feels them. I think that thinking these things somehow keeps me sane. There is something about memories—early memories especially—that beseeches us to stop and look. To keep looking. And to look again. Look at that cat, arching, writhing in the gutter, popped eyeballs flailing on strings, head bashed in. Whose is it? How did this happen? Or the high-spirited dog, shot and left to die in a field by the farmer with nothing better to do. Look at the boy, wild with passion and grief, striving to get himself killed. If you do not look at these things, surely you will become mad. I feel convinced that this is the case, but how true is it? Do you think such things? If not, would you describe yourself as mad? What if I were to not think about all this? Would it matter? Would I become sick to death? And if that were to turn out to be the case, would dying be so wrong, when to live is wrong? To *be* is wrong. How many people are aware of this problem? I doubt very many. Those who do know about it conceive of life as a trick of the light, as this allows for some movement in the face of disappearance. If you have found yourself rendered stateless or invisible, this fact is, as you know, of little consequence to anyone other than you and yet, paradoxically, it may bring ironic relief in that it offers an unusual freedom, if you remain willing to look. This freedom—an unexpected consequence of the trick of light—derives from what matters being thrown into sharper perspective. For example, you will know, or have experienced, even dimly, that there arises from within you, at the first glimmer of contentment and tranquillity, a distant howl of dismay: "Don't leave. Don't leave me."

The discovery and knowledge of your terror—that all you have striven for may lead to abandonment and death—can, surprisingly, bring consolation and relief. Your fear is that all you hold dear can, if ignored even for a moment, draw you into annihilation. Ignorance of the lasting influence of this fear is by far the greatest obstacle to freedom. Once unmasked as a fantasy of disaster designed to remind us of, not free us from, the past, contemplation of the disaster becomes possible. A more obvious example of the same enigma is contained in your fears about the future that paralyse your attempts to act for the best. Realisation that nothing that can befall us in the future will remotely approximate to what has gone before, may dispel this dread. What relief! How do you talk to a child about this? How do you *not* talk to him about this? Which words can circumscribe a set of circumstances located somewhere between invisibility and annihilation? Although it has been suggested that it is barbaric to write poetry after Auschwitz, some form of words that neither annuls nor reifies what has happened is necessary to free us from the unrelenting grip of these morbid ideas. Otherwise, the fact that being alive is wrong demands a renunciation of hope from the disenfranchised that cannot be given. What must then be embraced is the stench of the trace that now serves life's purpose.

It would seem reasonable to expect that subsequent memories might make the meaning of earlier memories clearer, but they don't, at least not in my case. Freeze-frame memories of the kind I have described—more like imaginings trapped in time than memories—are difficult to think about or to elaborate, compelling though they are, as there is no unfolding story, no narrative, just flashbacks of places I recognise but have never known. They seem like clips from an old movie, the plot of which has been forgotten. It doesn't follow from this that they are all necessarily bad memories. For example, I can picture a Welsh country lane, midge-filled in the summer heat of evening; or me throwing myself backwards into a cornfield, watching swallows tumble from a blue sky; or being fascinated by rabbit holes at the base of the oak in the woods where I spent most of my early years. The shimmering black mirror of a pond transfixed me with its beauty.

Around my third birthday my father arrived home one afternoon from his work as a window cleaner in overalls and trilby, and ceremoniously opened a newspaper-wrapped parcel in which lay a piece of meat. He held it out proudly for approval, fingering its tenderness, beads of sweat gathering in pools under his eyes. There was a second newspaper-wrapped parcel; another ceremony. He handed me a silver six-gun with a white handle: "There you are," he said, screwing up the newspaper. I thanked him, not knowing what to say, but feeling as though there had been a mistake. "Am I a part of this? Who is this for, and what am I meant to do with it?" I asked myself. In my confusion, I did what I think I have always done in bewildering or difficult situations, which is to walk away. It has always surprised me how little attention this gets. I found myself outside in the street dawdling along the pavement, which was skirted on either side by grass verges. I felt relieved to see the verges, unbroken, plain green, my cheeks brushed by fresh air.

The gun had two sights and was meant to fire caps. I came across some workmen digging a trench in the road. One of them looked up as I passed by, a knotted handkerchief on his head. I stopped and smiled.

"Would you like this for your son?" I ask him confidently, holding out the gun. He looked at it, then at the other workmen who had taken the opportunity to stop for a breather.

"Aye," he replied, grabbing it and pushing it to the bottom of his rucksack.

I walked on, feeling lighter, wending my way to The Woods across the ditch at the far end of the road. The Woods was my childhood sanctuary; my place, with what seemed to be a familiar but inexhaustible supply of experiences that stood for everything life at my parents' house did not. Long since submerged under cheap, modern housing, The Woods comprised a dark continent at one end (Asia and the East) and at the other a lighter, less sheltered area (Latin America, I worked out). Dividing them was an intermediate zone, roughly European and American, where I played for most of the time—amongst ponds, small animals and birds, tall and fallen trees and secret hideouts. There were battles to be fought, strategies planned and dangerous undercover reconnaissance missions to be undertaken. Regiments of loyal troops repelled invasions and liberated oppressed populations, after which they would enjoy well-earned recreation, mountain climbing, tracking buffalo with local Indians and digging for gold.

The sheer variety of natural forms in The Woods captivated me. I loved touching the dry, wet or frozen grass; watching the bulrushes rear themselves majestically in the Spring and then, unexpectedly in Autumn, shrivel up and disappear; following the leaf cycle in its million shapes and hues; the expanding frog-spawn that forced tiny, flitting sticklebacks into detours; above all, I was uplifted by the bright, exposing light of summer and its thrilling, slow descent into menacing darkness. The Woods was my home; a place of safety in which I was afforded a glimpse of what it might mean to do nothing. From the age of three or four, I spent most of my time in The Woods, leaving it reluctantly at night to make my way back to my parents' house. I think that if I could, I would have slept in The Woods. There wasn't a day when, it seemed to me, this well-worn retreat didn't look and feel different. Most of my time, when I wasn't exploring, was spent sitting or lying on a large, fallen tree trunk that straddled the main pond (the one that that transfixed me) on the far side of The Woods, at the edge of a cornfield. Whilst always a different place, nothing changed in The Woods, except the seasons. It was dependable and predictable. The trees, ponds and bushes took a neutral stance, neither rejecting me nor expecting anything of me. I was accepted.

There were times when being in The Woods could be lonely and threatening. One January afternoon I fell off the log into the pond. Recalling the practice of hanging out clothes on a line, which I'd seen done in gardens, I arranged my trousers, underpants, shirt and socks across branches and waited for them to dry. I hid in the hollow of a tree trunk. When I eventually discovered that they had frozen, I didn't know what to do. Could I put them on? If I did, I was certain to be punished. If I didn't, how would I get back? What happened next I don't recall, but I think I picked the ice off the clothes, put them on and waited by the ditch between The Woods and the road, where a passerby found me.

I tried hard and failed to put distance between me and these memories, ever-present though they are, making it difficult to feel them in any detail. They converge with earlier memories, as though my mind alters, compresses, re-invents memories: for what purpose? So I could survive? So I might die? I feel in these oppressive memories the familiar chill of a boy silently, anxiously waiting as his thoughts float off into space.

Most evenings, I meandered from The Woods to our house along the street past the primary school where I was later to become a pupil, following a ribbon of small, identical houses. Sometimes, I was drawn to yellow-lit windows that bathed the night, into which I would peep, partly to stretch out time and partly out of curiosity. My interest lay less in the people—I was afraid to look at them for fear of being seen and, in any event, whatever they might be doing held little meaning for me. I was more intrigued by the source of the warm, yellow light which I identified came from table lamps. This exotic form of lighting was new to me and had a powerful effect, rather like a later discovery I made that the cars I studied from the roadside transported entire families to remote, fascinating destinations. The cars flew by, their lines blurred, the occupants momentary, imaginary friends. I became preoccupied by the cars and their interiors, the snug, warm smell (as I imagined it) of wood and leather, animated families chatting into the night, the exciting glow of coloured lights, inside and outside, like a fireside Christmas tree. Occasionally, one car in particular would seize my imagination: for some weeks, a man drove by The Woods periodically in an Alfa Romeo Spyder. I imagined him to be a doctor. I went weak when I saw him and his, to me, exquisite silver spaceship. I studied as much detail as I could absorb with each apparition, drinking in the beauty of the car's gondola lines and his relaxed, kind face.

As an adult I never had hobbies, yet I could not shake off a recurrent interest in old cars. It transpired, to my surprise, that I could identify no single car, no matter how memorable or beautiful, that I wished to own. I couldn't understand this, as it seemed to me that no-one in their right mind could not fall for an Alfa, MG or E-Type. I realised that each car appealed to me only as one part of a larger jigsaw puzzle, and so could never, on its own, satisfy me. Individual cars represented particular childhood moments sitting at the roadside scrutinising passing cars. I collected thousands of registration numbers, reading up on them in a little book I had found. Thousands of trips made in hundreds of different types of car. Young people in sports cars, women out shopping in Minis, cheap family runabouts and fast, swooping saloons that whisked people to new worlds. All were important in formulating an impression of how people lived and I used them to assemble a composite picture of what family life might be like, in the absence of the experience itself. It became clear that I would need to own all of the cars if I were to feel that particular connection again and this was, of course, impossible. However, the cars I admired did have one thing in common: hope. Without realising it, I was imagining myself in these cars.

Table lamps were less complicated but no less convivial. After many decades, their subdued glow continues to awaken feelings of welcome and warmth.

Returning to my parents' house at night from The Woods, at a snail's pace, involved a series of careful detours and negotiations. Entering and leaving the house through the back door making, if possible, no sound. Taking, quickly and in large quantities, bread if it was out, butter or cheese or anything edible that I could eat in my room or the following day. A matter of priority was to avoid conversation. Steering clear of my parents was difficult, though less so with my father who was more of a lodger and whose routine barely varied. He left early each morning, before I woke, returning in the afternoon, drunk. He and my mother would fight before he fell asleep on the sofa. At nine in the evening they would fight again briefly and he would go out to the pub. Weeks, months might pass by without a word being exchanged between him and me. When he did speak it was at best monosyllabic, at worst scornful and humiliating, from which I shrank. When I spoke I was dismissed as "melodramatic". By this he meant that anything I said, especially if it contained enthusiasm, was the meaningless boast of a puffed-up exhibitionist, a conceited mummy's boy full of hot air.

I took this judgement to heart, but did not properly understand its origin until much later in adulthood when it occurred to me this was precisely his view of my mother's behaviour. He saw her as false and her family as pretentious social climbers, working class parasites searching for a host. They provided a counterpoint to his own family's unfounded snobbery. His accusation of falseness towards things I said had a confusing, undermining effect on the way I came to view myself and on the way I thought about thinking. I believed that whatever idea came into my mind it was, *de facto*, bogus—without meaning. What I thought or felt to be real or true was mistaken claptrap. It was a cunning way of invalidating my sense of who I was, as it avoided overt violence (my mother's preferred method) and drew instead on parental authority to poison an impressionable young mind, in the process making my father appear more reasonable than my mother. Two birds with one stone. His portrayal of me as melodramatic, combined with an absence of guidance about the world, settled on me as a "truth" for decades, filtering the things I said or did to leave me feeling insubstantial and inauthentic. In parallel to this was an equally abiding but different self-criticism that I associated to my relationship with my mother: a belief that my presence was toxic to other people.

My mother was more dangerous than my father, as her temper was violent and capricious. My younger sister, Patricia, and I were savaged by random, impulsive attacks that left us disoriented, shaken and eventually withdrawn. Most of the attacks were reserved for me, as my sister was crushed into submission at an early age and therefore easy to control. The rages seemed total, like a nuclear explosion that vaporises life all around. Everything changed when they happened: thinking, continuity and connection disappeared. Terror, paralysis and vigilance took over, in anticipation of the next attack which invariably arose when it was least expected.

I came to think of the element of surprise in my mother's attacks as the trait that rendered them especially effective, but as an adult I understood that what had appeared to be surprise was, in fact, an illusion. The attacks were driven by a quite different logic. My mother had a sixth sense for when we were off-guard or feeling a bit calmer or had got some enjoyment elsewhere, away from her and the house. It was these moments that triggered the explosions of violence. For no apparent reason, a hail of abuse would be unleashed that turned everything upside down, leaving me with a feeling that whatever I thought I had been experiencing, wasn't the case at all.

"You think you can sit around on your arse? What do you think this place is? A hotel? GET OUT!"

Humiliation seemed to be the objective of the assaults, and we were humiliated, but there was also something else involved. I understood this something else to be a detestation of the needs and feelings of children. My sister and I made demands on her that she felt were outrageous, unreasonable, impossible to meet and potentially highly damaging to her. We soon got the message that we were not wanted. If we ever forgot the message it was made crystal clear to us that we were pests, polluting and ruining her life. By the time I was four, I knew never to make any further demands on her and, wherever possible, to make myself invisible. The responsibility for this disastrous state of affairs with my mother I always felt was mine. Although forced to become grimly independent, I felt deeply ashamed at being a failure as a son.

My shame was the crucible from which my First Principle of life was born: *Everything I said and did was wrong.*

This Principle underlay the Second, Third and Fourth Principles, which I formulated by the age of four as strategies to deal with the consequences of the First.

The Second Principle was: *I do not believe what I am told. The truth is the opposite of what I am told.*

The Third Principle was: *Anger will keep me alive.*

The Fourth Principle was: *If I work twice as hard as anyone else, I might be able to live a life that approximates to a normal life.*

The experience of *being* wrong, as opposed to doing something wrong, corrodes hope. The truth eventually dawns, even on a young child, that if there is nothing they can do right they can either give up and commit internal suicide, as Patricia did, or try to overcome what cannot be overcome. I can only imagine it, but I suspect that many such children try to do both, as I did. I recall wanting to be dead from the age of four and I put myself in many situations where I might have died. At the same time, I tried to overcome the obstacles I faced. I was deeply, abidingly angry about what had happened to me, although I could not properly feel this. In the absence of a way to change my situation, I vowed to wait—to wait as long as was necessary—and to try to hold onto my anger rather than give up hope. This gave rise to the Third Principle: *Anger will keep me alive.*

At night, unable to sleep, my sister and I would sit on the stairs listening to my parents brawling. I wracked my brains for ways to stop them from killing each other, which was what I thought would happen, yet never did. My sister would sit behind me until it subsided, my father would slam the door and we would creep back to bed. These fights had a great impact on me, placing me on permanent alert. Over time, thinking about anything became difficult due to the emotional exhaustion and confusion brought about by the recurrent violence. I couldn't grasp the meaning of the fights or the accusations they hurled at each other: *"bastard... piss artist... cow... hewer."* I was to find out something about what these meant as I grew older, through the different men who visited the house whilst my father was at work. What I did know, however, was that the insults were filled with hate.

My parents killed my older sister, Carole. Born fourteen months before me, she developed gastritis after birth which went untreated. Eventually, my parents took their five month old child, now in a serious condition, to a hospital where dysentery was diagnosed. She died and was buried in a grave that my parents never visited. I discovered the whereabouts of the grave in my twenties, found it broken down and neglected, like its occupant, and had it restored. My parents could not discuss the matter. Later, when my mother's parents died, my mother arranged for them to be buried "on top of Carole", apparently to save money, and had the gravestone altered accordingly. When I discovered this, my mother would not discuss the matter. My father, an alcoholic and heavy

smoker, could not discuss it either as by this time
he was dead. He had died of lung cancer, aged
fifty-six.

Let me put a question to you that is more important than the tawdry behaviour that led to Carole's death. Why did this woman, my mother,
have children? More specifically, after failing to
sustain the life of a healthy, newborn baby, why
did she go on to have another, and then another?

Convention may have played a part. Aspiring
to the appearance of a settled life in the late 1940s
and early 50s for working class people, meant
middle class possessions that smacked of family,
stability and happiness—a job, house, children, a
television. These were the trappings of normality.
This was probably the case for her. Also, young
married couples who did not bear children ran the
risk of being stigmatised as infertile. However,
these factors do not on their own account for the
need to create and destroy life on such a scale.
There was something else.

My mother was afflicted by an abiding sense of
injustice. She believed that she had been cheated
out of everything that was rightly hers. Having
met her mother, a sanctimonious, ruthless woman
interested only in herself, I can imagine a basis for
her grievance. The consequence of my mother's
disenchantment was that she grew to believe she
was entitled to anything she wanted, which she ra-
tionalised on the basis of a fantasy that she was superior to other people. So strong was the belief
and the airs and graces accompanying it, that
neighbours and relatives came to refer to her as

"the Queen". The reality of having children and a day-to-day family life appalled her. The obligations involved came to feel like perverse demands that depleted and demeaned her. She felt dragged down into ordinary life with its dreary, small-time pursuits that she had long ago renounced, and she fought back tooth and nail using contempt, self-aggrandisement and sex.

My father's life was destroyed long before his cancer finished him. A beaten circus animal, he paraded for anyone who would watch the one trick he'd mastered—pouring the tincture into wounds that would never heal. By contrast, wormwood destroyed my mother's life. Hatred, guilt and disdain accompanied her loyally to the last, whipped up by an assortment of pariahs that persecuted her. The neighbours, her husband, me, her daughter—anyone who needed her became the object of her scorn. Together, my mother and father destroyed the marriage they went into, the children who came out of it and their own lives. One child killed by neglect; two soul-murdered and starved, not simply of food but of the nourishment that makes the difference between a human life and feral existence. Their own relationship atrophied within months, from which time on they were estranged occupants of the same house, my father drunk and my mother pursuing any man who she thought might gratify her need to feel valued.

The thankfulness and sense of release with which both of them greeted their final illnesses made the end of their lives easier than anything that had gone before. The prospect of a swift despatch, through cancer and a stroke respectively, brought uncharacteristic peace to both of them. Death had been the lodger in our house, not my father.

Wrong

It is difficult to know what motivates individuals to desecrate everything they might otherwise hold dear, but it is not be impossible to imagine. One reliable, albeit uncomfortable, source of understanding lies in ourselves. Our uncanny capacity to reproduce our parents' characteristics, sometimes in fine detail, will, if reflected upon, yield valuable information on ways in which we were treated, how we responded and how we turned childhood adversity to seeming advantage. Our most private desires, our wishes to hurt and degrade, our notions of dignity and shame, all took root in the longings we harboured to love and be loved by these, the most important people in the world. Their beliefs inculcated in us and moulded an enduring need to pattern ourselves after them. Ironically, it is in our most determined efforts to never repeat the folly of their ways that we reveal the depth of our complicit pact. The same may apply to our choice of spouse.

A common rationalization for the origins of this transmission and repetition of character is what lies behind aphorisms like *"plus ça change"*, or *"like father, like son"*. Whilst true in a general sense, these sayings overlook in their simple fatalism the irony that each hapless, subsequent instance of repetition arises in a quite new and different context, and could therefore be said to be without precedent. We are confronted in adulthood, at each turn, with the audacious fact that our belief that we are the sum of what has passed before, is a fantasy. What do we do with this remarkable news? Nothing; at least in my own case and my sister's and, I suspect, many other people's. For years I clung to the belief that I was normal (whilst feeling that everything I did was wrong), that my parents' behaviour was explicable, that my confusion was due to an aberration on my part and, above all, that despair never touched me. Despair afflicted people at the bottom of the heap, not us. Evidence that I was spawned from this heap, as were my parents, and their parents before them, was lost on me, even though it piled up before my eyes. Perhaps the truth needed to be lost on me: greater awareness of what was taking place and the fact that it almost certainly could not change would have been too much to bear.

One of the starkest pieces of evidence that I was wrong, one which is beyond a child's capacity to assimilate, was my "badness". My mother's malice was directed towards a "badness" in me which seemed to consist of an inhuman, disease-like quality that she both reviled and feared. Not only could I not offer her anything, the sight of me made her sick, as though she was being threatened by contagion. What this badness consisted of I didn't know, but of its existence I was in no doubt. It was communicated to me sometimes by physical beatings but more often by verbal missiles:

"How DARE you do that, you stupid IDIOT!"

"You make me SICK. Get out my sight before I give you something to cry ABOUT."

"Don't come near me, you little bastard. Get OUT!"

Words, no matter how accurate, are wholly inadequate to describe the shame of daily, weekly, monthly humiliations of this kind, year after year, from the age of one until I was able to leave home at seventeen. Their impact was global and diffuse rather than specific—like a climate that shapes received opinion rather than traumatic memories. The words carried by the missiles were often not understood by me; I don't think they were meant to be. I recognised the use of everyday language, but it was delivered in such a way that a response was out of the question. How do you behave on hearing "'Eyy, YOU!" launched in apoplexy from nowhere? Its aim was to shock and paralyse, rather than to communicate, and this was achieved by instilling in me fear for my life. It was the force of the laceration, as much as the content, that stripped me of a capacity to defend myself, with the result that I quaked whenever she became enraged. The combination of terror, disorientation and physical pain at being screamed at (cramps, asthma, night terrors, incontinence) immobilised me and crushed any resistance.

Although I tried to remove myself emotionally when the assaults took place by imagining myself standing outside my body, this was not successful. As long as I was visible I was wrong and a target. Her spleen pierced the core of me, pitching me into quicksand. Waiting for the turmoil to end became the only course of action open to me. I succumbed to the tirades as something that I had no choice but to live with, which meant accepting that every next step or moment, within me as well as outside me, courted disaster. The First Principle was created to explain this.

Why did she treat us, especially me, in this way? This question is difficult to answer, as motive, character, background, prevailing circumstances and the relationship to the particular child, all need to be taken into account. The task multiplies in size when the fact that a third of UK children report witnessing, or being the recipient of, parental violence (physical, sexual or emotional abuse), is added into the equation. In addition, every perpetrator is different, which means that a separate, detailed inquiry into the circumstances of each case is needed if the truth is to be ascertained. Obviously, themes emerge, as anyone who studies the literature on child abuse can discover, but they do not convey the experience of the child involved. In my case, piecing together what happened took a long time, involving many detours, mistakes and unfinished ideas. With help, I reached what was, for me, a convincing explanation of my mother's behaviour and my "badness". This was not an academic exercise. I had always blamed myself for what had happened—*everything* I did was wrong. My need to find out why I was so wrong was for my sake, as I simply could not fathom why my belief about my badness was so gripping and enduring, despite my efforts to dispel it. I also knew that many of my parents' accusations were not true. I developed my Second Principle because their attacks seemed to turn everything upside down. The Principle was: *I do not believe what I am told. The truth is the opposite of what I am told.*

I felt fairly sure that my mother's upbringing was wretched. They lived in extreme poverty on Merseyside and she resented it, always aspiring to something better. Yet this is no crime. The source of her bitterness about people and, later, her madness, seemed to lie in the emotional poverty of her upbringing. Something happened between her and her mother at an early stage in my mother's life that alienated them from each other for ever. The consequences were disastrous. As a small girl she would run away from home, often taking harrowing risks. She became sexually precocious in her teens, pursuing boys and men in order to prop up her fragile self esteem, so poor was her relationship with her mother and family. As she grew older she invested wholesale in men to try to meet all of her needs, and in the process elevated herself to the status of Queen. She acquired a husband, a house and children which, for her, were trophies that distanced her from her past. Inevitably, she could not mourn the death of her first child, so decided instead, on the advice of the local doctor, to replace her with another one, as you might a broken vase. A year after Carole died, I came along.

The reason why my mother did not savage me from the word go, and why I did not become schizophrenic, was due, I suspect, to the Miracle of Resurrection. As if by magic, when I appeared, she discovered that her baby, her trophy, had been restored to her, just as the doctor had said would happen. Here was dramatic evidence that there had been no death, no loss, no missing little girl. She had come back, with no recriminations or blemishes. It took her some time to grasp that the store had run out of the type of vase she had previously bought and had instead sent a different design—a boy, not a girl. Within a few months it became clear to her that she had been grievously wronged. The wrong baby had been delivered. Its existence was testimony to the fact that the magic, the miracle of Resurrection from the dead, had not worked. He was *the wrong one*.

When she tried to look into the baby's eyes to find the matching gaze of her immortal daughter, I imagine that she was confronted repeatedly by an indictment that a child, a healthy little girl, had had her life and prospects destroyed desperately early. So great was the scale of the destruction that it could not be contemplated, yet this is precisely what this new, unwelcome arrival seemed to be inviting. The situation was not helped by the dreadful mistake having needs of its own and making demands on her to have them met. A symbol of death and debilitation, not of life, had been imposed on her, and she hated it. Not only did the blunder of delivering a boy have nothing whatsoever to offer her, it taunted her with the failure of the plan that was meant to put everything right. After trying and failing to clothe him in a dress, she had to do something to rid herself of the cruelty of the accusations. It was too late to send him back, but by having nothing to do with him she might go some way towards reversing the events that now tormented and haunted her. She erased his presence. He was to be disowned and forgotten about. This is the reason why I was wrong and bad. I did not *do* anything wrong. I *was* wrong. The arrival of Patricia three years later made matters worse, not better, as by then it was too late. Her dead and living children had ruined her and her husband had turned out to be of no help whatsoever.

One consequence of being seen as a girl from birth in this way and then discarded was not that I felt like a girl, or became gay, but that I felt like no-one at all. My mother saw someone else when she looked at me. I felt that I did not exist. This is not the same as feeling insubstantial. I became aware, as many children do, of not being up to situations: speaking, mixing, playing and later working were all difficult. I am referring to a chasm in which I floated, miles above earth, with no knowledge of the language or customs below. Existing in a void with few coordinates renders meaningless almost everything other than physical survival. Human contact, play and the wider world were of no interest to me, not because I rejected them but because they were incomprehensible and irrelevant to survival. I became a creature of The Woods, a little Victor of Aveyron, where I found solace and felt, for the most part, unthreatened.

I had been killed, like Carole, the distinction between us being that my body remained and hers didn't. I knew this to be true, but I could not think about it. I knew I ached and that I was hungry all the time. I knew that every day would be the same as the one before. I learned that no-one knew or appeared to care about what was happening to me or Patricia. There were times when I thought I could reverse reality (hence the Second Principle) and made strenuous, repeated attempts to get through to my mother, despite the onslaughts, on the basis of an idea that she might be amenable to reason if only *I* provided it. To prevent herself from being contaminated, my mother needed to ward me off in any way she could. She did it by screaming or walking out. With Pavlovian repetition, I tried to get around these rejections using reason. If I failed, which I always did, it didn't matter: I could always try again another time in a clearer way, expunging any hint of offence or claim, in the belief that she would eventually see sense. This was a very serious error of judgment. It did not work; not once. As it was the last line of defence in my rag-bag armamentarium, I could not afford to let it go, there being nothing else. I persuaded myself that she *must* understand—one day—even if I had to give up hope for now. I drilled myself into believing that by setting a fine, rational example, even though I would need to remain silent, I *would* connect with her. In other words, I went mad.

Being reasonable and unfailingly helpful became a character trait, emerging automatically in my dealings with people, particularly women. The secret of getting ahead, I came to realise, lay in self-abnegation, identifying the other person's wishes and meeting them. Providing attention, interest, flattery, reassurance and unsolicited offers of help put me ahead of the game. The potential for misunderstandings, conflicts and self-betrayal in this delusional way of life was enormous. For example, as a young man, I once befriended a young woman and then refused to allow her to leave my company until I "explained my position", which took two hours of haranguing of which she understood nothing and that left her deeply distressed. I had replicated with her a version of the way in which I had been harangued and tortured.

By conspicuously appearing to grasp what other people wanted whilst remaining invisible, I was oblivious to the fact that I was metamorphosing into a husk, a circus animal like my father, performing tricks on the basis of a tacit belief that, despite their superficiality, they would ensure my survival. I concealed carefully any need for people, cultivating an impression of independence. I turned tricks into real life, and real life into a sham. I found myself excluded from life on the inside as well as the outside and was inevitably confounded by how or why people related to each other, seemingly so naturally:

"Hi there. How are you? What have you been *doing?*"

"Where did you go on holiday?"

"Now, can you write a story, perhaps about the place where you were born?"

"What can I get you?"

Listening, responding to and spinning out conversations were enigmas. Why *did* people say these things? Something about it must appeal to them. Even if conversation did mean something, why was it needed in the first place? From my retreat of confusion and compliance, I became hardened and apathetic towards listening and speaking, as I knew I had nothing to offer. My words were ciphers that recycled other people's ideas: clichés best forgotten for the detritus they were. Why exhaust myself? Behind my burn-out and isolation lay a harsh reality: I was unable to think. The struggle to keep up the idea that making connections was no problem had served to divert me from this disturbing fact, and from facing a further truth that might have spelled the end. I could not love or feel loved. Suicide began to play on my mind at around the age of four. I tried to imagine what it might be like to be dead and how to make it happen, but the closest I could come was to lie on my back in The Woods petitioning oblivion. Nearly freezing to death by the pond, walking casually across busy trunk roads and responding to any stranger without a trace of anxiety could have provoked disaster on any number of occasions. My actual death seemed to hold less trepidation than what had already taken place. I was a terrified, broken child with the daring of someone who had nothing to lose and who cared only for primitive survival. At times even this could lose its urgency.

I recall once hearing my grandmother remark: "That boy... he goes where angels fear to tread."

I didn't understand her comment at the time but, as it had an impressive ring to it, I took it to be a compliment. It seemed that I had the capacity to do anything I liked. Nothing could stop me. I did not know that she was referring to my headlong, reckless daring. This behaviour was fuelled by a disregard for life and by an idea that I could find something better. Where the idea of something better came from was a mystery, until I understood what my mother had given me, unbeknown to her or me at the time. Her inability to accept Carole's death provoked in her a brief reaction to a short-lived miracle when I appeared—the Miracle of Resurrection. I had, understandably, misread this reaction as love for me. Whoever the child was my mother craved to find by looking at me, I was the child on the receiving end of her gaze, at least for a while, and this confusing state of affairs spared me from outright rejection and probably psychosis. By showing me what it was like to have her baby back, I was given a glimpse of faith in the possibility that there was something good in life. Faith is the belief that some good will happen, without necessarily experiencing evidence to support the belief. Trust comes with personal experience of the evidence. I never experienced trust, but I did experience faith, and it was from this that, I believe, the Principles were able to emerge, along with hope that something better existed, some-where. If something better did exist, there was at least a possibility that I might share in it. I have al-ways been grateful for this.

SCHOOL

Although I had begun at times to feel suicidal, fear prevented me from killing myself. Instead, I killed time. My movements grew sluggish. I no longer had anywhere to go, so could go anywhere I liked. I ambled to The Woods, lay in the grass or wandered the streets for hours to delay my arrival at the house. I would summon up a vision of rest, of lying peacefully, quietly, perfectly still; no people, no noise, no sound, not even breathing, just the caress of cool, fresh air, a pastel sky and silence. Sometimes, a lullaby I had heard my father sing to Patricia after coming back from the pub, drifted in the breeze:

We're poor little lambs
who have lost our way,
Baa Baa Baa,
We're little black sheep
who have gone astray
Baa Baa Baa.

Gentlemen songsters off on a spree
doomed from here to eternity
Lord, have mercy on such as we,
Baa Baa Baa.

By the time I began primary school at five I could find myself in this dream place several times a day. On days when I was unable to summon up up the dream images and felt low, often with aches and pains, I would push myself into sleep by going off to my hiding place at the base of an oak in The Woods. When I felt the pains coming on, sleep was a priority, whatever time of day it was. I practised falling asleep until I could do so on command, more or less, when I was alone. I would look forward to bed, as entire stretches of time could be erased. Even a whole day prior to sleep could be made to disappear, for good. By the time I awoke to a pristine, featureless morning, the past was ancient history and I could make a fresh start.

My gait slowed further when I began school. I took a lot of time, as much time as I could, walking, waiting, postponing arriving and trying to merge myself with my surroundings. I often imagined myself concealed by or camouflaged in The Woods, indistinguishable from the bark, leaves and shadows (the initial spur for this was an army of threatening Orientals stationed on the far side of the fence between The Woods and the corn field, which I needed to avoid). Gradually I extended the camouflage to include hedges, grass verges, walls, the school buildings, the classroom, even the air itself in the classroom. I didn't need to join in with people. I was concealed and invisible. I was a ghost.

All the while I felt in charge of the power to alter my form and vanish, I was unaware that I was trying to make myself undetectable to my mother. The stark fact that I had been defeated and had no resources left to resist her had extinguished any hope of connection with her. I had only one option: to avoid the savagery that proceeded as usual. The idea of continuing life with her became overwhelmingly difficult. The prospect of life without parents, whilst impossible, seemed the only course of action open to me. I embarked upon a strategy of fading away, of effacing myself to a point where, if possible, I was unnoticeable at any time, day or night. I craved to be alone.

It is ironic how much effort it takes to make a non-existent person invisible. To achieve isolation requires discipline. Where isolation wasn't possible I had to find ways of creating isolation in the presence of others. I discovered forms of behaviour and words or phrases that had the effect of deflecting attention away from me. Saying and doing nothing was quite successful, as was replying with: "I don't know", "I didn't understand" or "I'm sorry".

Sitting at the back of a class or on the edge of a group could achieve anonymity. Not turning up at all was the most effective method. It was rare that anyone noticed and this became my preferred approach. It took time to hone being absent-present, as the most challenging aspect, particularly in school, was to ensure that other people didn't come to think that I thought they had nothing to offer.

There came a point, a few years later, when I believed, wrongly, that I had succeeded in effacing myself. We were set a test at school as a trial run to sort the wheat from the chaff in order to decide who would go on to the better grammar school and who would go to the inferior secondary school. The entire event was lost on me. I turned up at school as usual, saw on each desk an identical piece of paper with a list of questions, sat down, wrote some answers and after twenty minutes or so wondered what to do next. I was bored, and as the room was quiet, I slipped out on the pretext of going to the toilet. I headed for The Woods. No-one stopped me as I sauntered through the school gates. I was free! The thought dawned on me that I could come and go as I liked. I could simply cut my ties with school. I needed space to preserve some peace of mind, rather than exhaust myself figuring out how to be in the class. Discovering that school need no longer matter took a weight off my mind. I did not connect my departure that day with what occurred some weeks later when the class teacher, an angry man called Mr Adamson, strode in one morning in polished, cracked Oxford brogues and dark, shiny suit to make an announcement of the results of the test. Mr Adamson had always disliked me, I think because he thought I refused to cooperate, which may have been the case. He boomed: "I shall read the results of the test in order of merit."

This meant little to me. I wasn't sure what merit was, or what test he was referring to, so I listened with scant interest. I became a little apprehensive as he read out the score for each pupil, each successive mark being lower than the previous one, without my name coming up. Did it matter? I recalled vaguely a test for the "big" school, but I couldn't remember it or what I'd written. What had happened? Maybe I hadn't been able to do it. Had I been absent that day? His voice slowed: "Fletcher, 65. Green, 62. Johnson, 56. Kimpton, 50. Simmonds, 48... Meredith, 43..."

I began to quake, as he was nearing the end of his list and my name hadn't come up at all. He put away his papers and stood in front of his desk holding a sheet of paper before him.

"WILLIAMS," he barked.

I jumped out of my skin. In a flash I realised I had scored no marks at all. My results were the worst in the class. Or maybe I hadn't done it when I should have. He strode between the desks toward me, grinning. It was a grin I recognised. My mind began to race. It was over. I would not get through this. I would leave the school. To calm myself, I repeated the thought that I could get to The Woods soon and things would be better. He stopped next to me and slowly placed the paper on my desk. I flinched, urine trickling down my leg. The silence shrieked shame.

"Eighty two, " he declared, to everyone and no-one. Spinning on his heel he strode back to his desk and sat in silence, staring ahead. I didn't understand. The class, and he, were now looking at me and had begun to laugh. At what? Some children started a slow hand clap. What for? I was a stray dog that had wandered in and was being told it had won a greyhound race. They were laughing at my stupidity. Still racing, my mind decided that it was all a joke. I sensed anger again and this calmed me a little, getting me back to the idea of going to The Woods. As suddenly as it had all begun, it ended. Adamson waved the class to be silent and began a lesson, none of which I heard.

BADNESS

There are drawbacks to being a ghost, despite its advantages. It reduced my fear of people by making them less important, but I could not have predicted the increase in the "badness" I felt. What contact I did have with people became more, not less, shameful, leading me to shun them further. My "badness" could take the form of an idea that my body was ugly—fat, deformed, grotesque—and that my internal organs were decomposing.

Everything I said and did was bad. I contaminated people, animals, furniture—anything I touched—and could detect disgust in people's lowered eyes as I passed by. I feared their anger and contempt, but more than this I feared exposure of my putrescence to public gaze, and the instinctive, sterilizing backlash that would follow. The more I hid, the greater my aversion to being shamed. A version of the badness that defined me seemed to have affected members of my mother's family. My father often verbally attacked her and her family as a debauched group, preoccupied by sex, drugs and indolence. My mother seemed unable to defend them; nor did she attack his family. Her method of defence was to attack the individual with maximum cruelty in an area of vulnerability. I came to see this as her first principle of survival (the second being sex). His drunkenness and neglect of her were the green light for his humiliation.

He: "Get back to your bloody relatives, you lying, rotten whore. You're all the same. Scum. They've never worked a day in their lives. I've got more in my little finger than the whole rotten bunch of you put together."

She: "Who are you to talk about my family, you drunken bastard? Leave them out of this. If it wasn't for you we wouldn't be in this mess. You piss away every penny there is, treat this place like a hotel and expect me to be here. You pathetic, sick bastard. Fuck off."

He: "Here we go. Listen to this... Lady Muck! Who do you think you are, you trumped up little tart? You do nothing! You ARE nothing. You're all the same."

And so on. These rows were structured along two lines: first, the badness each accused the other of possessing and second, class difference. My father had come from a better-off family (his father had started a small window cleaning business which my father drank away) whereas my mother's family were mostly unemployed, from the poorest Merseyside working class. She married my father hoping for a leg up the social ladder. I had heard her boast to neighbours of the house my father was brought up in—furniture, table-cloths, crockery, etc. It must have held out the prospect to her of a different world from the one she had known, where poverty, inhumanity and cruel humour prevailed. The badness she saw in my father was his false superiority expressed as contempt for her and almost everyone, and the hypocrisy of this. She countered it by reducing him to a pathetic, cardboard figure. The badness he saw in her was a sexually degenerate self-obsession in which she wallowed shamelessly. My mother's four siblings (she was the oldest) had varying degrees of the disease. The least affected was Jim, the youngest, who had more or less escaped stigmatization because he was a quiet, teetotal man who had lost his wife to kidney failure shortly after their marriage. Jim turned out to have a post-traumatic psychiatric condition that left him withdrawn and isolated. Buddy, born next and deemed a lost cause, especially by my father, was an apparently dangerous, uncontrollable street fighter with supposed underworld connections, a gypsy wife who was a prostitute and children who weren't his own. I heard that he fell off a ladder and, paralysed, killed himself with a heroin overdose. Chris, next in line, was a hail-fellow-well-met with a smile, girlfriends and a drink and joke for everyone. He could not take anyone or anything seriously, became alcoholic and died young. Kitty, my mother's only sister, was dismissed as insane and degenerate by both my father and mother, as was her husband Bill, along with her children, especially her Down's Syndrome daughter, Janet. To my ill-informed eye, Kitty's family stayed together and seemed happy enough.

My father had two siblings, Grace and Lucy. Grace was a short, gargantuan lady whose size was explained as being due to "glands". She had married an old, thin, man, Poppy, who lived upstairs in their dainty semi-detached house. Poppy, a crooked, professor-like figure, wore several cardigans and seemed to hover half-way up the stairs calling for Grace. Occasionally, Grace invited me to visit her house. It was a wonderland of pink sofas, small tables, rugs, china ornaments and doors that opened onto a perfectly trimmed garden, with bird boxes on each tree.

"Paul, darling, now do come in and sit down here next to me and let me get you something. How are you, dear? Poppy is having a little nap, so you and I can have a talk, can't we? Now what would you like? A glass of milk? With a biscuit? I know, what about a little something that usually only grown ups drink, but I'm sure you'd like—a nice cup of sweet coffee made with lots of frothy, hot milk. Wouldn't that be nice?"

"Thank you, yes."

I was dazzled by Grace, the opulence, her *joie de vivre*, her biscuits and her cup of sweet "Camp Coffee", a black liquid made of sugar, chicory, coffee and water which she mixed with boiled milk and served in a white china cup and which I invariably spilled, flooding the saucer. I'm not sure I liked it, but I drank it because it, and everything about Grace, epitomised ease and refinement. While she prepared the Camp Coffee, I would stroll around her little dining room gazing at my reflection in the polished table, fingering candlesticks and exploring a sideboard that contained cutlery, a tray and a decanter. I pressed down on soft, bouncy carpet, stroked the heavy curtains and studied her glass ornaments. There was a barometer in the hall. I had seen nothing like it.

"Paul darling, coffee's ready. I'm just taking one up to Poppy and we'll have ours together in the sitting room in a jiffy. Do you like ginger biscuits? I do hope so."

Despite the sumptuous surroundings and her generosity, I found I could not relax with Grace, as conversation was very difficult. It was not her fault. She was a kind, effusive woman, albeit a bit odd. She enjoyed telling me about my father who, she assured me, was one of the most intelligent men she had met, and that he had captained Wales at football. It was my fault Grace and I couldn't get on. I had no state of mind, no vocabulary to make sense of her interest in me. My inability to chat in such uncharted emotional territory made me witter on the sofa in a vain effort to appear normal. The stress of trying to talk, together with a worry that I might spoil her pink chairs, led me to stay away. I did not want to stop seeing her, so stole some biscuits from her kitchen on my final visit which provided a reason to not return.

I came across my father's other sister, Lucy, only once. She was a haughty woman with a Liverpudlian BBC accent and brilliant children at university. She looked down her nose at me. This was the extent of our contact, or almost. On my father's deathbed, I noticed a woman silently busying herself with the sheets and tidying his bedside table, without looking at the visitors.

I thought at the time she was a nurse, but discovered later it was Lucy.

One person in my mother's family seemed to have escaped the degenerative disease—her father, Charlie. As with Lucy, I barely knew Charlie. He ran a large pub called The Glue Pot in Netherfield Road, Liverpool, which was too far for me to visit regularly, but I did go once or twice and discovered that it had a system of underground caverns filled with dozens of wooden barrels that had been rolled down from the street by the brewery dray. My mother's brother Chris chased me with a hosepipe around these cellars, to my delight. I would watch Charlie skilfully "tap" the barrels when he needed to send up fresh supplies of beer to the bar. A roar in the copper pipe attached to the barrel's bung hole signalled the gurgling up of beer into the hand pumps in the bar above, ready for siphoning into glasses. Jugfuls of creamy froth were drawn off before the amber liquid emerged clear.

I remember Charlie for an unsolicited act of kindness that stood out in my early childhood. I must have been crying and had shuffled into his pub office, which was a dusty attic room containing a table and beer crates for chairs. I hadn't expected him to be there. He came over, sat down beside me and put his arm around my shoulders,

saying: "There   now,   Paul.   Don't   worry.
Everything's going to be all right."

No-one had said anything like this to me before. At first I felt like crying again, but then I felt
better and stopped. I was very grateful to Charlie,
although I barely saw him again.

LIES

Ghosts are meant to be invisible. I became a ghost because everything I said or did was wrong, and I could not bear the shame of it. No retreat was far enough. I was made of the same stuff as my mother and father. They hated themselves, each other, their children and their lives, so it was inevitable that I would feel that there wasn't a shred of goodness in me for others to recognize. I needed to conceal the disgrace that I had failed as a child. My shame could not be exposed under any circumstances. When a fox is run to ground, to be dug out by beaters' spades in order to let the hounds in, it is a fate beyond contemplation.

I may have believed I was invisible, but I still needed to shun contact with people. This included expressions of affection which produced a pain that confused and frightened me. The fear of exposure of my shame and fear of being wounded by affection could generally be held at bay by remaining isolated. However, ghosts suffer from an unrequited wish to make contact with the living, as well as a need to avoid them. At primary school I found, to my alarm, that there were times when I would feel an irresistible urge to talk. At these moments, I metamorphosed from a ghost into a jack-in-the-box, spouting outbursts of gibberish. All of a sudden I would talk nineteen to the dozen, under the illusion that I was like everyone else. I had no idea why I did it. Decades later, Patricia came across primary school reports for both my father and me, when each of us was six years old. Despite the thirty years between them, some of what was written was almost identical. One sentence appeared *verbatim*: "Generally good and quiet, but has an occasional tendency to talk too much."

I think my need to talk came from a longing to be like other children. It was a submerged hunger that took me by surprise, as for the most part I felt unbothered by any such need. I was a withdrawn, solitary child ("generally good") but there must have been times when I succumbed to the enthusiasm of other children, to the sunshine, or to some other allure that weakened my resolve to stay invisible. When I did talk, I painted an admirable picture of myself and my life. This was a ridiculous thing to do and, of course, I was at sea as to how to achieve it. I engaged in knowing mini-monologues on subjects the teacher had asked about, in the hope of appearing to be a good pupil. I gradually learned to bring these baroque outpourings to a close quickly, in order to avoid humiliation. The effect of my odd interventions was to lift my self-esteem through a temporary feeling of inclusion, without uncovering my "badness". My homilies bore some resemblance to the efforts I made to get through to my mother by setting a fine, rational example, whilst having to remain silent. They were crazy.

When threatened by shame, I would lie. It was of the essence, when lying, to convey something good about my life that made me seem like a normal person.

I didn't have anything much to go on, so lying became a logical necessity. I was unable to make up stories about my mother because I couldn't think of anything good to say about her and, as I had not had much to do with my sister Patricia, it didn't occur to me to include her. My father was, up until I was four, a remote figure, which allowed me to build some intricate fantasies around him. Also, the fact that I barely saw him made me wonder what he did. I imagined him as a ship builder on the Mersey, commanding a loyal army of workers. Or as a celebrated inventor of a device that prised barnacles from the hulls of ships. I didn't wait to try to convince others of my ideas, as well as myself. My tales about him faded with the beginning of his accusations of melodrama. Grace could occasionally be brought in as evidence of my breeding, and, as I was captivated by different forms of transport, especially cars, I could use my knowledge of these, mostly without a need to lie. I did not discuss The Woods or nature, as these were private.

There was a lot at stake when I resorted to lying, as the aim was to ensure that I eradicated any outward trace of the shame that infested me. It was important that neither I nor the person I was trying to impress questioned my story, so the magnitude of the lie had to reflect the degree of secrecy being maintained—in other words, how much I was threatened with exposure. Such a threat did not need to be external. There were times when I felt so unworthy, so despicable, that a lie could start within me purely to counter my self-loathing. I might then enact the lie. For example, I did not feel able to participate in any group of children or adults. When I imagined trying to join in, pressure would mount in me, particularly if I was, in reality, welcomed, to a point where I would lie to people about the area I lived in, my background and my family (in order to conceal my origins) despite the knowledge that some of those I was lying to knew where I came from. It was my own self-hating state of mind that needed to be assuaged.

It is possible to make belief in a good lie so self-evident that neither explanation nor justification is needed. However, it is a dark art that can unravel if taken too seriously. I took lies very seriously. The tales I told could have been exposed easily (and probably were), so it is clear that the person my lies were designed to deceive was me. Escaping the truth of my situation as a child was critical, but I was unaware that the price I paid for a life of fabrication was my sanity. What prevented a descent into full-blown psychosis was, I suspect, the sanctuary of The Woods, faith, sleep and the formulation of the first Four Principles.

The lies I told had a positive effect on my morale that was instantaneous, and this allowed for a swift withdrawal without shame. The lies came in two versions: minor and major. Minor lies were reflexive responses designed to present myself in a good light and avoid being singled out:

"Yes, I understand."

"I *did* read that."

"No thanks, I'll be having something when I get home."

"I don't have a bike; it was stolen."

These small-scale falsifications were enough to hide everyday reality and could bring conversation to an end quickly. There were a lot of them, and on the surface they contained little substance. There was a side to them of which I was unaware, and this was that, sometimes, they conveyed unwittingly the truth of my situation. For example, "No, I don't have a bike; it was stolen" wasn't true in an objective sense—it was a lie, as I didn't have a bike. But as there was no bike, no childhood and therefore no child to ride a bike, the bike I was referring to could be said to have been stolen from me, along with the entire experience of growing up. With hindsight I began to see that, despite my efforts to conceal my disgrace, I was probably communicating it inadvertently on a regular basis. It is surprising that not more people noticed. Perhaps they did, through their unease with me, which I experienced as a familiar response to a strange, troubled child.

Major lies tried to impose an entirely different reality onto my own. For example, my parents might be talented and rich, I might live in a different city, even another country, have ancestors I could trace back generations, and so on. It was not always easy to keep major and minor lies apart. There was an occasion, much later on in childhood when I had turned twelve, when I blurted out a small scale lie that spiralled out of control, exposing a major lie that threatened to undermine all my efforts to avoid shame.

To try to be like other people, I had joined a local amateur dramatic group of children and adults from the school and surrounding area. They were performing a musical play, and I and another boy from my class were down to perform a short, uncomplicated dance across the stage. I made a reasonable job of it, after many unsuccessful attempts. Following the public performance of the show there was a get-together in a hall. In large gatherings of people I would feel anxious, as too many things seemed to be taking place at once. This expressed itself as a physical tension that left me drained. I did not know then that children who spend their childhood as I did experience fear in their bodies, like a permanent electric current. I had got so used to it I thought it was normal. In large groups the tension caused me to freeze and my recourse was to leave, or steel myself until I could get to The Woods. People were milling around the room when, suddenly, a piano struck up and everyone began to sing the Beatles' song *Yellow Submarine.*

The realization that this was a party—a place to be *happy*—hit me with the force of a hammer blow.

Disoriented, I found myself sobbing during the singing, without knowing why. I could not stop myself, which humiliated me, and a concerned woman came over and helped me out of the room. One of the male school teachers who I had admired from afar, Gerry, joined her. They took me into a side room and sat me in a chair.

"What's the matter?" she enquired in a kind, concerned way.

I didn't know what the matter was and was unable to speak for crying. As they watched me the convulsions gave way to a feeling of pressure to explain and justify myself. I was so thrown by my distress and the spectacle I had made of myself, that I found myself saying: "The farmer shot my dog."

They looked at each other, shocked.

"That's terrible," she said. "When did this happen?"

"Last week," I stuttered. "I was playing in the field behind our house and he... he shot him."

"You poor thing..."

Their concern for me made me want to cry more, but by this stage I knew that they hadn't understood. I hadn't understood. There was no dog, and no farmer. I had no idea why I had said what I said. I had lied unthinkingly. I needed to reel in the lie as quickly as I could, but didn't know how to do it, so insisted that I was all right and ran out, heading in the direction of The Woods.

The shame of what had taken place tormented me to the extent that only one course of action seemed possible: to confess to these people that I had lied, apologize and ask them to forgive me. I didn't know who the woman was, but I found out where Gerry lived, took some change from my mother's purse and went on the bus to find his house. I found it, knocked on his door with foreboding and was welcomed by Gerry who showed me into his sitting room.

"Paul! Come in. I was concerned about you. How are you?"

Unable to contain myself, I poured out my confession and reasons for having lied. As I didn't know what they were, my jabbered attempt to redeem myself must have sounded bizarre. Gerry's face began to darken.

"Paul, you do know it is wrong to lie, don't you?" he asked.

I replied that I knew that to lie was wrong and pleaded for his forgiveness, promising never to do it again. I was talking ten to the dozen, reiterating my apologies. At that moment the most important thing in the world was that he did not think badly of me.

"That's enough, now. I think it's time for you to go. Are your parents outside?"

Gerry stood up and walked towards the hallway. I followed him, beseeching him in a way I can't recall having done with anyone.

"What's done is done, Paul. I think it would be better if you left."

I tried once more, but he led me quietly out onto the garden path and closed the door. Gerry and I never spoke again, despite my being a pupil at his school for five more years, and I never understood why. He was not a harsh man, although at the time this is how I thought of him. Later, I began to think that he may have felt out of his depth at having to deal with such a disturbed, unintelligible child.

I also never understood why I had told them that a farmer had shot a dog I didn't have, until I realized that I was the dog.

HUNGER

By the age of five I had developed what today might be called an eating disorder. I devoured food, eating large quantities as quickly as possible, to the point of inducing nausea. I would then "forget" to eat for a day or two, sometimes longer. I also "forgot" to drink. I rarely felt thirsty and if I did drink it was usually very little. I couldn't see the point in drinking unless I was extremely thirsty, which wasn't often. Food was another matter: hunger could quickly become painful and this was a continuous risk as we did not get regular meals.

My voracious eating was also designed to protect myself from disappearing. At a certain stage of hunger, I would become concerned that I would no longer be able to fill the space I occupied. I became convinced that if I allowed my size to shrink any further I would fade away and vanish altogether. At these moments, I was overwhelmed by a craving to eat, as though my life depended on it. The source of this fear of rapidly petering out derived, I think, from moments in which isolation coincided with feelings of hopelessness about my situation. I lost any basis on which to proceed, and went into a sharp decline towards severe depression, which generated panic. I would experience myself as ceasing to exist. I felt I was watching myself die and there wasn't another soul aware of it. I had to save myself. Occasionally, the fear of dying took the form of breaking into pieces and floating off into space. By forcing food into me, I could do something to maintain my size and shape, and stay on the ground.

Fear of dying by vanishing was an unintended consequence of my resolution to become invisible, in order to make myself undetectable to my mother. The original decision was taken as a way to avoid being savaged: the less she saw of me, the safer I was. I had acted according to my First Principle—*Everything I say and do is wrong*—so invisibility was the soundest, most logical defence I could construct. It was a blanket strategy that infiltrated, like bindweed, my dealings with everyone, culminating in a philosophy that left me permanently marginalised. My core view of my mother as a capricious tyrant came to taint every person I met, causing me to shrink from human contact in anticipation of condemnation and humiliation.

By the time I was five or six, a further eating anxiety occupied me. I came to think that I was huge—fat, ugly and intrusive. Entering a room became an ordeal. Being photographed at school had to be avoided. Eventually, being seen at all felt impossible. I stopped eating altogether in the presence of other people due to my belief about my size. In order to eat it became necessary to hide, so I sank into the peacefulness of The Woods, playing for hours in what felt like the nearest I had experienced to freedom, eating when I wanted to, in practice quite little. The threat of shrinkage and disappearance, or of appearing huge, seemed to lessen so long as I remained in The Woods. When I ran out of supplies, the prospect of contact with people frightened me. I fought the fear and left The Woods covertly to seek out food and gorge, and once sated, I retreated to my sanctuary. The belief that I was huge seemed to be a variation on my need to avoid human contact. It embodied my fear of conspicuousness and the savagery I imagined would follow, and had the effect of smothering any need for others that arose in me.

I devoured mainly bread when I was hungry. Even if other things were available, I didn't eat them, except for butter or cheese if it was available. My selectivity didn't make sense, as when you are famished there is no time to discriminate. You need food fast and as much of it as you can get—even if at the time it makes you feel sick—in view of the uncertainty as to when you will eat again. It is also unwise to refuse food when it is offered, the exception being if it is inedible. Following the same uncertainty principle, if food is left out it must be taken at once whether you are hungry or not. If you don't take it, the *fear* of starving, as opposed to starving, may become overwhelming.

I saw bread, butter and cheese as accessible, quick-filling foods—they could be taken from a carving board, fridge or any work surface. They needed no preparation, created little mess and could be carried and stored for days. Butter melted so of the three was the most dispensable, but the other two were reliable and unaffected by the seasons. Once oriented towards a basic food supply in this way, survival seemed possible. I knew bread was a staple food, so that even if there was none in my parents' house, I might find it elsewhere—stacked up against a shop before opening time, thrown out at the end of the day or in a shopping bag hanging from a pram. It was not easy to steal from strangers as I was afraid of getting caught, but I overcame this fear. Milk bottles on doorsteps were convenient, provided I rotated the houses I selected. I recall, at the age of three, using a tricycle to collect a dozen or so bottles of milk from nearby houses, for storage in The Woods. Milk's easy availability and pre-packaged form made it as convenient as bread or cheese.

These foods had something else in common, which helped explain my selectivity. There was a minimum of human involvement in their preparation, or at least that is how it seemed to me. Neither of my parents was interested in cooking, and when they did the results were so unpleasant that they put me off prepared food for many years. My emotional response to the meals they produced played a central part in my revulsion: at the same time the meals themselves were inedible. My mother had a recipe which she used once a week

or so to produce a hot meal. It was a stew consist-
ing of pieces of mutton boiled in water with car-
rots, and flavoured with tomato ketchup. The
resulting orange-grey, fatty mess became emblem-
atic of all the things I couldn't swallow about our
lives. I had no choice but to refuse it. I did try to
eat it but vomited, and subsequently vomited at
the thought of it. Battles over eating it didn't last
long. My refusals (I would rather have died than
swallow it), my vomiting and my mother's futile
rages at what she saw as my ingratitude were too
much for both of us, leading to a stand-off.

I did not eat food my father cooked either, but
for different reasons. He fried food with fingers
that were grimy and nicotine-stained, and I feared
being poisoned. He had a habit of shitting himself
when drunk, leaving his trousers stained and
stinking. He rarely took a bath, which added to the
stench, so I avoided anything he touched, including the lavatory seat, but especially food. I did not
feel with my father the need to vomit as I did with
my mother.

Smells played a part in guiding me away from
danger as a child. Fresh air, rain, grass, leaves, the
scent of blossom and petrol fumes were comforting smells (to this day I can't sit in a car without
opening the window). The aroma of bread from
the baker—in those days it was made locally on
the premises early in the morning—produced a
heady optimism at being away from the house.
Odours of beer, shit, urine, over-cooked food,
cheap perfume and molasses (pubs in those days
had sawdust on the floor and a jar of molasses on

the bar which, when mixed with beer, acted as a sweetener and laxative) made me heave. My aversions intensified as I got older and broadened to include forms of behaviour that I found repellent, such as arrogance, effusiveness, displays of generosity and expressions of attention, including sexual interest in me. I did not understand the nature or intention of people's contact with me, and could only imagine it to be hypocritical and ultimately cruel. I also anticipated being shamed and humiliated by accusations of melodrama, and I read each encounter accordingly.

I had given up expecting anything other than hostility from my mother by the time I was about three. I tried to take an interest in my father up until I was four or so, in the hope of finding something, but without success. His drunkenness and scorn pushed me away. I tried sniffing his clothes in my parents' bedroom in the hope of getting to know something about him, but it had the effect of making me feel sick. Although I knew that neither relationship was viable, and as a result renounced trying to make them work, I could only continue to function by holding onto some sort of picture of my parents, and this meant my father. To make him more acceptable I got rid of who he was and re-invented him (and by extension all men) as a socialising, voluble chap, like a drinker in a Hogarth cartoon. The skewing of reality required to sustain this image created far-reaching damage. I grew up attributing false merriment to social gatherings, a falseness which I took to be true. I was lonely, confused and unhappy, in contrast to "normal" people able to enjoy themselves with ease (an ease I took to be false but which I nevertheless envied). I tried to act like them, but the more I acted the more I felt like a performing seal. Perversely, I was reproducing, in a false way, something that I believed (falsely) to be false. When the strain of acting became too much I collapsed into depression for which I savaged myself. I had little insight into any of this until adulthood, and could see no alternative way of being. I viewed myself as a freak whose manager was a clown available for performances on demand.

The assumptions I had made about basic foods like bread, butter and cheese—that they were not produced by human beings—were clearly wrong, as all three require people to prepare them, as does even a natural product such as milk. Where my confused logic did make a certain sense was in the idea that those involved in producing simple food had not allowed themselves to take centre stage, eclipsing the food by their personalities. Unlike my mother's stew or my father's fried cooking which were contaminated by who they were, the producers of bread, butter, milk and cheese remained anonymous and in the background, allowing the food to speak, or taste, for itself. No-one, it seemed to me, had interfered with the food to spoil it. The discovery that certain food might be unadulterated took a momentous leap forward when, as a teenager, I went to live and work in France. There, I encountered Norman peasant cooking: baguettes, cheese, fruit, butter, cream, cider, fried chicken, vegetables. If there is such a thing as a trauma in reverse, I experienced one. Day after day, for two years, I got drunk on simple meals prepared from natural, fresh ingredients. It was an experience that changed my life.

As a child I ate alone, unable to sit at a table with others. I acquired a see-saw pattern of gorging on leftover or stolen food, interspersed by periods of not eating or drinking. No explanation for this erratic behaviour was needed as no-one noticed or cared, which also meant there was no backlash. I managed to escape eating any meals in the house. Sporadic eating at speed, alone, became an established pattern, so that later, when I was required to eat with people, for example at school, I became anxious, gobbling and finishing meals long before anyone else. I was stared at and teased. Sometimes, a school bully might bump into me, causing me to drop my plate, or spit in it when I wasn't looking. I didn't react, but simply looked to the ground to hide my shame. I had the mark of the deprived misfit, the black spot, that attracts predatory malice, and I felt this disgrace was my due.

To try to fit in, I decided to copy other children's eating habits. I didn't know how to use cutlery, which provoked amusement, so I forced myself to slow down and scrutinise others. Although I mastered the basics of a knife and fork, I just couldn't eat normally or at a regular pace. In confusion and frustration, I quit eating at school altogether, which was no great loss. The food wasn't good—overcooked stew, grey cabbage and waterlogged pie with lumps of custard—and I got away from the teasing and bullying. I embarked on finding food elsewhere in the middle of the day, which was an activity I was experienced in and which also allowed me to eat alone.

Trying to copy the behaviour of others in order to fit in, as I did, is resorted to by children who have had no upbringing. A child raised by humans acquires templates for social behaviour based on personal experience that people engage with each other, including at mealtimes, and this is what gives life meaning. The to-and-fro of feelings, conversation and touch between people progressively fill up a child's world inside as well as outside. A picture of life unfolds in different colours, but colours that are mixed according to the minds, personalities and ideas that permeate the child's universe. This transforms the biological child into a human being. Faced with the colours of life but no means of recognising, mixing or using them, the deserted child remains shackled to primitive ways of thinking. Anxious to be in the world but checked at every attempt, such children dispense with trying to grow up normally and opt instead for magical solutions to problems they should never have to face alone. An illusion of knowledge and power takes the place of realistic thought, and a system of smoke and mirrors is instated whereby making things happen merely requires wishing them into being.

Imitation is the method used to perform this infantile magic. Normally, babies take their first psychological steps by imitating their mothers as a bridge to finding their idiom for living. An infant who cannot trust his mother or father, who lives permanently in fear and who sees the world as a place that threatens him with psychological or physical death, cannot outgrow imitation and evolve into an independent person. No idiom for living develops, and the infant comes to rely upon imitation, abandoning its own personality in favour of a performance that may last a lifetime, polished and honed as circumstances dictate. Without colours, palette or picture to draw upon, there can be no knowledge of how human beings interact and no incentive for talking. The child's needs and anxieties can't be negotiated, and a mirage of confidence is conjured up by wishing into being a life of imagined normality. Suddenly and miraculously, anything I need can come to pass because I make it available—in my mind. This new-found power means that I can be normal, live in the real world with others and do what I want, when I want. The idea that such a child lives in the real world could not be further from the truth, but can you conceive of a more compelling way of deceiving yourself and those around you than by investing in a carbon copy of life? In one fell swoop, past problems and their crippling legacy are consigned to history.

The more that imitation and performance displaces a child's personality, the more unbalanced the child becomes. Beneath false hopes, optimism and compliance lies a sea of desperation and confusion, the concealment of which compounds the child's feelings of inauthenticity and shame. The child feels under tremendous pressure to pound the performance into ever smoother shape, so that it may become difficult to distinguish between it and the actions of a natural, unbroken person. So taxing is this effort to sustain sham spontaneity that the child's capacity for interaction of any kind is, in practice, extremely limited. The mental and physical exertion of performing a role, and the fear that at any point, the entire edifice might collapse and disintegrate leading to exposure and catastrophe, are too much for body and mind to bear. The organism becomes susceptible to illness, and the mind splits and fragments itself to survive.

After years of rehearsals and thousands of performances to different audiences, dread of being denounced and shamed hardens into contempt as the grown-up child routinely and emptily delivers his pantomime act without feeling, assuming the identity of another person as casually as borrowing their pen. To attain this predatory skill the child must be able to recall a myriad of phrases and behavioural cues and learn to reproduce them in salvoes that carry conviction. Why human behaviour takes place and what links one piece of behaviour to the next must never be thought about, as this risks triggering the confusion and hopelessness that underlies the child's predicament, leading to depression and paralysis. It is no exaggeration to say that the child's mental and emotional resources are consumed by the need to dedicate each waking moment to scrutiny of and adaptation to others. When alone, rehearsing the performance remains a preoccupation, strategy upon strategy being concocted to prevent unmasking of the artifice. Even in dreams, illusions of plenty, greatness and happiness can fill up the mind to counter nightmares of emptiness, bankruptcy and abandonment.

The process of losing yourself to self-deception takes a long time. What starts out as a struggle to survive overwhelming events by hollowing out the mind in search of a bearable reality, culminates in dread of the truth and allegiance to subterfuge as the mind is filled with illusions and lies. By the time I was two, I was immersed in a life and death hunt for a place of safety. By four, I had withdrawn into a private world in which other people played little or no part. By eight, my years of seclusion and the fact that I had received no parenting resulted in a permanent break from almost everything human. A person in such circumstances scavenges for life with minimum visibility. Nothing is desired, desire having no purpose. Reflexes animate the hulk that replicates the movements of an individual, and mental intelligence that has gone to waste is recycled as fuel for the sideshow that passes for sociability. I knew nothing about life. However, I had learned about death. I knew that an attempt was being made to kill me, and that I was not the only target. My sister had been killed and my parents were engaged in killing themselves, each other and, if possible, my surviving sister. Nothing mattered but to withstand this threat, even though I might die in the process. If I did die, at least it would be a death of my own making. Troubles with eating, school bullies, social humiliation and exclusion, whilst distressing, were manageable compared to the threat of death. I saw them as prices to pay for survival.

An irony for the adult who has embraced a life of performing in order to remain invisible is that he must continually persuade himself that he is succeeding, if he is to keep mental illness at bay. In so doing, he unwittingly renounces his freedom by underwriting a life of hell for himself. Trapped in a costume, steeped in scripted lines, he drags performance after performance out of his human remains, each spectacle tearing strips of flesh from the little he has left. He has no control over what he says or does. His talk is mechanical and involuntary and his movements those of a puppet. Like a toy that cannot be switched off, he struts the parade ground, fending off foes and oblivious of the humanity of anyone he meets. They are all the same. They are all out to kill him.

DRUGS

In some Nazi concentration camps, the skin and fat of Jews was used to produce lampshades and soap. In some ordinary houses, the minds of children and infants are cut open to sluice away barbarity and depravity. Savagery towards infants does not account for all the ills of childhood. Things can go wrong for children for a wide variety of reasons, but the murder of souls and sometimes bodies is more widespread than is realised and its occurrence is typically denied. Ordinary people simply aren't capable of such things, after all.

The average German was drawn to the ideology of Nazism as a panacea for the ills of a sick society.

Ordinary, decent people embraced cruelty with fervour and a clear conscience, the superior cause of social purification providing justification. Although their behaviour was insane, they themselves could not be said to have been. They were systematically seduced by an ill group into succumbing to a delusional solution to a complex crisis that invoked the magic bullet of extermination. Theirs was a disease caused by Jews, Gypsies, Blacks, Homosexuals, Liberals and Intellectuals and all they stood for. Once the source of contamination had been identified, the cure was clear to everyone. The pestilence had to be slaughtered.

Children who are unwanted are demanding, useless pests who destroy freedom and opportunity. They add nothing to their parents' lives and rob them of what they do have by their self-centredness, attention-seeking and petty needs. Having to deal with this outrage is an abomination and an abuse of the parents' time. These vermin must be eradicated. If the creatures are fortunate enough, they may survive by scavenging for scraps like yard animals. Should their judgement desert them and they ask for something, they soon discover that their existence is a privilege, not a right, and that if they take advantage of their parents' generosity in putting up with them, they can be disposed of. If the parents care enough, they may excoriate them into understanding how the notion of "rights" does not and will never apply to excrescences like them. Crudely enlightened, the children learn to be thankful that permission to remain alive is not withdrawn.

These are the social circumstances, so to speak, of the bacillus that blights the parents' lives. Insult on this scale must be repulsed. This is accomplished by neglect, intimidation, verbal assault, physical attack or, in some cases, murder. There is no place for sponges that leach valuable resources by interfering with the parents' pursuit of pleasure. The parents are preoccupied in pleasuring themselves, there being no pleasure to be had in others. Sex is significant in this (as is drink), but not the type of sex commonly referred to as lovemaking. It is sex that patches up maimed self-esteem and inflates punctured vanity.

SHE

Her concentration camp life on the back streets of Birkenhead taught her to be an expert in catching the glint in his eye that he wants to fuck her, fuck her and be done with her. She feels a radioactive cloud pulsate through her ravenous flesh, confirming what she knows. She is the one, the sole object of desire. She is the only thing on his mind. She is *special*. Like a mother gazing at her new born baby, he takes her in as he rehearses the fuck and she feels complete. She lacks nothing. With this knowledge comes something every bit as arousing: power. She concludes that cunt rules the world. Like a credit card with no limit, it can get her anything she wants and transports her from the concentration camp to paradise. She relishes her sexual prowess, hoarding it and wallowing in its effectiveness. She has him where she wants him, when she wants it. She can tell him what to do and, like a puppy, he obeys, including fucking off.

With power comes control and she senses new possibilities. If she can have him where she wants him, when she wants him, why not the rest of them, in whatever ways she chooses? There are so many bitches and bastards to deal with; so much that has prevented her from having what she wants. Why can't she cut through the lot of them and get it now instead of wasting her life, like the arseholes all round her? She finds the weak points in everyone: her mother's envy and contempt; her father's inability to say no; her sister's self-hatred that makes her a soft touch; her youngest brother's drug habit that connects her to powerful men; her eldest brother's fixation with being charismatic. With practice comes the ability to charm and intimidate almost anyone. She comes to the conclusion that the vast majority of people are pathetic, hiding their fears and self-loathing behind do-gooding disguises. A stare or sharp word is invariably enough to bring them to heel.

If they get above themselves she can cut them down to size whilst making them feel she is doing them a favour. Power is intoxicating. At times, she feels unassailable. She invests each waking moment in building up her cunt power base and new, wider ambitions grow in her mind. She wants continuous pleasure. She wants independence. She wants money. She wants freedom. She wants nobody.

Children are persistent swine. They hang around, whinge, want to be fed. Their belly-aching, cocky ideas of entitlement, snivelling demands and above all their inability to show gratitude, threaten to suck her dry. She needs to get the fucking message across—shut the fuck up and fuck off. It takes time, which annoys her, but she does not shirk from the responsibility, shrieking full tilt when they open their foul mouths. They can be devious in trying to get round her but this serves only to make her more determined. She lashes out, pinning them to the ground. She doesn't want a fucking thing to do with them—ever.

Get it?

Things get quieter. She barely sees them. There is no comeback. She forgets about them and concentrates on the business of pleasure. Cunt, dick, feeling special and powerful. She is on her way to getting everything she has ever wanted. On the back of her triumphs she resolves to procure what she wants faster and more efficiently. The focal point remains, as always, the pulsating, radioactive cloud that unfurls with the drooling gaze. This she must not part with, as this is what got her to where she is today. There is no reason why, having identified the source of power, she can't exploit it for her benefit by scoring quicker and more frequently. She organises an assortment of packages and doses of pleasure to suit her different urges. Slow fucks, quickies on the run, cunt, dick, finger, wanks in a warm bath. The dicks also give her gifts: a necklace here, a nightdress there. Even a holiday. There are nights out: *go on*, it's a bit of fun. Tipsy, giggly, wobbly, quicky. They pay her; why not, for Christ's sake, she's gone without for long enough. She comes to realise that they can afford more, particularly the anxious prick with the wife in the next street. She's in business. The

heady thought dawns that by cultivating independence without dispensing with any of her
pleasure, she can do what previously she could
only imagine—build a capital base that could set
her free from all of them, emotionally, financially,
the works. They could become her customers, em-
ployees even, as she finds new ways to use them.
She might finally rid herself of the piss-artist who
stinks out the house. She could then make
something of the place in the way she wants. The
possibilities are endless. The little bastards who
try to ruin her life won't get in the way.

The power that derives from amassing cunt
capital takes root in her life and mind. So busy is
she that she barely notices how the emphasis on
pleasure shifts imperceptibly but steadily to *entitlement*. There is no reason on earth why, if she
puts her mind to it, she can't have everything she
wants. There are no limits on her imagination.
Obedience, compliance and capitulation are the
qualities she looks for in others, as she diversifies
into new sources of pleasure and capital. She starts
a small business—hairdressing—and employs a
meek, dutiful girl to shampoo, rinse and sweep
up. She enjoys telling her what to do. The place is
spotless and she concentrates on her customers.
She is a determined, attentive hairdresser who
knows how to put the customer centre stage. Before long, the money is coming in.

Calculated orchestration may be the driving
force behind her capital project, but she is surprised to find that there are moments when talking to her customers is enjoyable. Unprepared for

these, she catches herself wondering whether one day, her life might work out.

She watches the clock and finishes promptly to get herself ready for pleasure. One rule she makes for herself is to spend nothing when she's out. The dicks quickly got used to providing her with treats and, progressively, etiquette hardened into formal protocol as treats became mandatory. They are, after all, privileged to be with an exceptional, desirable woman who only asks for a few little comforts. Alert to new derivatives of pleasure, she notices how desire and expressions of esteem make her feel the radioactive cloud, but with a twist. She can now feel special and powerful at one and the same time. This cocktail is similar to when she comes and her mind explodes with glittering fantasies of castles, fireworks, flattering princes, snow and servants prostrating themselves. As he fucks, she wants him to tell her she is the most beautiful, glorious fuck in the world. She demands long awaited recognition that she is The Queen.

What she despises most about children is their weakness. They have no power, yet think they are entitled to everything. She despises her customers for a similar but opposing trait: fawning inferiority that prevents them from ever getting what they want. She mocks the laughter and chatter she hears on her nights out as pitiable escapism. She finds evidence of powerlessness and weakness everywhere and will not be sullied by it. The more powerlessness she comes across, the more determined she is to acquire the respect she deserves. So mired in their impotence and lack of vision are people that they don't seem to recognise her obvious qualities. Even the dicks come up short. She begins to have to point this out to them and it annoys her.

Increasingly frustrated by her parochial surroundings, she refines her assortment of pleasure-power packages into concentrated doses by cutting out the frills and foreplay. She wants distilled praise and excitement on tap, irrespective of the messenger or context. She takes to phoning the dicks and getting shot of them when she's done. . She can't tolerate the disappointment at being kept waiting or spoken to without flattery. When she feels mistreated, frustration torments her.

Demeaned, she is consumed by humiliation and clamours for redress. Do they not know who she is?

She has pruned back her customary conviviality into a more hard-nosed formula for getting what she wants. Her skill at smiling, telling funny stories, reporting scandal and making attention-grabbing generalisations has acquired pin-sharp focus. She now insists upon praise and sexual attention. Compelled to scan each encounter for its promise and drawing on her guile to seduce and cajole, she succeeds more often than not. She feels intense relief, like alcohol or heroin coursing into the veins, and this gives way to a glow of pain-free contentment. The experience may last for an hour or two, sometimes a day, but it wears thin under mounting inner criticism of the inadequate fools she has to depend upon for her happiness. Their ugly, babbling faces dance before her, leaving her disgusted. Criticism is directed at herself for being so senseless as to imagine that these half-wits would ever be capable of giving her what she wants. If she fails altogether to elicit praise and sexual attention, the rage that swells in her like fresh lava galvanises her into a determination to get what she deserves from these imbeciles once and for all. It is at these moments that she turns to her children, and this is when they are most at risk.

HE

By contrast, he neither understands nor is interested in sex, and has only ever thought of it as an obligation, like needing to pay for a drink or having his haemorrhoids fixed. He never understood the role of dick she requires him to play but is willing to go along with it, be flattered by it even, up to a point. He gains little pleasure from sex due to the effort involved and it soon turns into play-acting. He isn't interested in masturbation either, except when sober and depressed, which is rare. As with everything else in his no-man's land, he needs to be drunk to function.

So despicable does he feel that he restricts his activities to simple things that carry a low risk of disgrace. Cleaning windows, smoking, making small-talk, drinking beer and whisky. At a certain moment the pain of his debasement, soothed by drink, is edged aside by a fantasy that he is a confident, well-liked man whose company is sought by others. He smiles magnanimously, buys the drinks and repeats improbable stories that gain attention. He feels he is among friends. The pints merge, and he drifts into a peaceful, tearful backwater. He is at rest. His glazed, chemical respite is not enough to anaesthetise the rat in his stomach or the voice in the back of his head that speaks to him.

"He's still here. Who do you think you are? Do you think you can get rid of him? Come on now. Don't be a fool. Accept how things are."

Unnoticed by him, at the precise moment he felt calmed by the alcohol, the rat began to gnaw at his stomach lining as though begging for food, and he becomes distracted by what appear to be important worries regarding things he needs to do. He has difficulty identifying what they are, as they swim together overwhelming his mind, with none standing out as a priority. They clamour for attention like orphans. He is in less doubt about what he is beginning to feel—a familiar burden of unidentified but stifling responsibility that settles on him as he bids his comrades farewell with a noble sentiment: he has a family he must see to, like any husband and father. His friends nod their understanding and they part emotionally, a few minutes afterwards sharing confidences about his decency, generosity and affability. As he steers his old car home, using the kerb as a guide, he clutches for his peaceful backwater but it has turned to boredom, listlessness and an impression that everything he looks at through the smeared windscreen is the same, pallid colour of concrete.

The drive is too long. It seems to go on forever and he fights to keep his eyes open, even though it is mid-afternoon. Nauseous, he drifts into surveying his life but his thoughts are patchy, present troubles and overused memories rubbing shoulders in a tired haze. He thinks again of his friends in the pub, unsure as to why he couldn't stay. Why did he leave, like he always does? He is not interested in the answer. What comes to mind instead is the bare, cold house to which he feels no more attached than a flop joint. He feels a need to get away from it, even though he hasn't yet arrived. His prehensile wife flits in and out of his vision, and he feels unsettled. He can think of nothing to say to her and decides he will sleep when he gets in, like he does most days. He knows it will inflame her. Fuck her.

He wonders half-heartedly about his life. What does it mean? What is he supposed to do, for Christ's sake? The accusation lingers in his head for a brief moment before he turns on the radio. A crooner burbles a romantic ballad and his miserable curiosity is replaced by absorption in how he might handle himself when he gets to the house. He will not let her push him around, so he'll stand firm and keep her in her place. He doesn't have to put up with her. He is worried by the thought of confronting her, even though he thinks about it every day. Nausea creeps back into his throat. Is he getting sick? He doesn't believe he is. The tincture of alcohol and bile reassures him that this is a small price to pay for peace. He begins to feel on safer ground towards the journey's end, his priorities having become clearer in his mind. He *needs* to see his friends for a drink. It is the one time he gets to himself and he is going to keep it. There is nothing to compare with being stoned, motionless and smiling. As far as she is concerned, she can put up with it or leave. He entertains the thought of living without her, a thought he also thinks most days, and sees few difficulties. He begins to feel more confident and at ease. He has her where he wants her. His home is his castle and he can do what he likes in it. Anyway, they get on all right most of the time as they hardly see each other. His apprehension allayed, he looks forward to putting his feet up and his evening in the pub.

He could pass for breezy as he greets her before lying on the sofa. She ignores him. He ignores her and sleeps. He ignores his children. They study him from a distance to gauge the danger and then retreat. It will not be long before the fighting starts. He sleeps, dreams fitfully, snores and farts leaving no room in the house quiet or untainted. The children gone, the scene is set for the fighting, their surrogate for sex, which will take up the evening until he leaves for the pub. The children will see themselves to bed. He is curiously energized by these rituals, as they underscore the distinction between life with her and time for himself in the pub. She is unreasonable, hateful and utterly predictable, whereas time with his friends is an oasis of camaraderie, civilised conversation and peace.

The fight takes its unfailing, obnoxious course leaving them hate-filled, temporarily guilt free and persuaded afresh that they want nothing to do with each other. He puts on a white shirt, the one he has worn all week, tie, shit-stained flannels and shiny blazer and marches parade-ground style to his comrades who await him. Drinking itself, for him, has comparatively little to do with enjoyment, despite outward appearances to the contrary. His joviality is sustainable only in the context of a broader strategy that seeks to keep his body anaesthetised by alcohol as far as possible without having continuous access to it. He needs to paralyse his feelings. His drinking might best be thought of as a medical procedure for the inducement of coma, his preferred state. Uninterrupted consumption of beer and liquor in varying quantities and proportions delivers him into a trance. He will need to factor in periods between drinking bouts, so he builds in a reserve to sustain a scaled-down version of the coma until he resumes the following day. A general, guiding principle is to drink until he feels he is on the point of being unable to stand, and then merely sip. He sometimes overshoots his target and has to be carried back, but generally he manages a passable walk, collapsing into a dreamless, comatose sleep without the need to undress. He wakes a few hours later pain-free, still drunk and changes into his work overalls, takes a cup of tea and is away before anyone else is up.

He has learned from experience that a dwindling trance allows him a few hours of energy for work until the pubs open at eleven o'clock, at which point he finishes for the day. In fact, he has made it his general business to clean the windows of pubs and moves from one to another during the morning. He puts on an air of being particularly busy and does not like it if this fails to rouse the attention of someone indoors. When he is noticed, his affability spills over and, although the pub is closed to the public, he is invariably invited in by the landlord for a quick one, on the house, in recognition of thirsty work. He selects his pre-eleven o'clock pub on a rota basis and so gets to properly drink in a variety of surroundings each week. After the windows are done and he has settled in the bar on his own, he stays until closing time at three. People he knows come in and out and greet him. Although he never refuses their company, privately he prefers to drink alone.

He does not eat, relying for calories on two pints of stout at one o'clock. As his anxiety levels lessen so the solace of the coma beckons him to the balmy, tearful backwater and all is once again as it should be. This is not a feeling of happiness; it is an emotional vacuum in which behaviour that seeks to express what it is to be human—feelings, thoughts, engagement with others, plans, work, dreams, activity, pleasure—is extinguished. His fervent wish is to become inhuman and to stay that way. To be without feeling and turned so deeply into himself that nothing impinges on him. This has come to represent, for him, life's purpose. By reducing his vital signs of life to stuporous quiescence, he is able to maintain his inhumanity for stretches of time that meld into a semblance of permanence. His apparent gregariousness camouflages this deadly activity. He has lost awareness of how galled he is when obliged to be animated with people, his reflexive and inexhaustible bonhomie betraying both his ignorance and the degree to which he no longer recognises himself.

He has never felt human because he has never loved anyone and has never felt loved by anyone. He has occupied the margins, watching and imitating others, acting the part, keeping up with each round of drinks no matter how much he vomited in the lavatory. One of the boys. There isn't anyone with whom he drinks who isn't convinced of his generosity, comradeship and wit. He, by contrast, is strung out, disconnected and threatened by everyone, unless drunk. His body is a mechanical device with which he feels no kinship and he has taken to observing it and fearing it, as one would a zoo animal, lest, or in the hope that, it might behave unpredictably. His mind, such as it is, seems to control him to the extent that his time is spent either chasing its peculiar demands or retreating from it in search of respite. When feelings temporarily get the better of him, as happens with the first or second rush of drink, he can deliver a well-developed line in derision that dissects witheringly anyone or anything displaying integrity. His passion is reserved for degrading anything that is honourable so that it is smeared by his philosophy of faeces. He mixes a potent cocktail of sarcasm, condescension and sadistic humour which he finds works well in most situations, but is especially effective on children. When they show interest in anything, or laugh, or say something fanciful in the way young children do, or when they become distressed and need a parent, as his own children at times inevitably did, he takes lascivious pleasure in lining them up in the way a hunter might take aim at sitting ducks. With exquisite timing he waits until they are at their most exposed and dependent and, with devastating effect, rips out the child's feelings and fills the void with an injection of faeces designed to shame the child into ever having imagined that their concerns were of the slightest interest to him or to anyone.

These are the most satisfying kills. More mundane attacks take the form of mockery of a class-based strain aimed at ridiculing anyone who comes up with a hope, plan or new idea. He has identified a universal tendency in people to get above their station, and he knows this has to be punctured if they are to see the world for what it is and get shot of their phony, elevated views of themselves. It needs to be made plain to them that they are no different from him and the most effective way of doing this is to finger them and their fraudulent aspirations for the melodramatic flim-flam they are. He loves to watch the expressions on others' faces as he lampoons their deluding, self-promoting fantasies with sly, malicious wise-cracks. The target is not merely the aspiration itself but the state of mind that enables a person to believe that they have it in them to create or merit something of value. His drinking pals see his cruelty and contempt as a branch of waggishness that you shouldn't take too seriously. Saner people who don't know him find him coarse and insulting in a depraved way. His children view him with fear and suspicion. The impact of his mendacity towards his children has instilled in them a belief that any ideas or thoughts they have are invalid because they would be, by definition, the product of vanity. The effect of believing that you are capable only of showing off undermines imagination and sabotages the development of a sense that you are a person with a right to think and feel. If all you can do is posture, what does this make you? He will tell you: it makes you into a two-faced, arse-licking piece of shit that can be seen through a mile off. His children despise themselves. They feel they should be dead yet must carry on behaving as though they are children, knowing all the time that they are filthy, pointless scum. They believe that every cell in their bodies is made of faeces, but faeces of a uniquely foul and shame-ridden kind that no-one knows about except their father and mother.

There are occasional, rare moments during drinking sessions when he begins to feel himself transcending his burdens and moving into a zone of pleasure that is different from the backwater he usually reaches. This place seems to contain infinite possibilities: he feels he can do anything and with this confidence comes an uncommon feeling of exhilaration. What brings it on isn't entirely clear. He can be feeling sick of life and at the end of his tether or, paradoxically, it can come out of an opposing feeling that he is an admirable, rather special character who is handling the world pretty well. It manifests itself in a heady self-belief and a feeling that his capacity to drink is unlimited. He drinks very heavily whenever he drinks, but this is different. In this state of mind he can pour infinite quantities of alcohol into him without feeling unsteady, befuddled, sick or sated. It is as though there is a boundless, empty reservoir within him that could take weeks or months of delicious, sweet-tasting drink to fill. His behaviour at these times is assertive; he cracks jokes, he has a sparkling answer for everything and he dispenses advice with the omniscience of an old hand. He buys the rounds, holds court and declines offers of help to get home. He feels stupendously, aggressively in charge. His opinion of people at these times divides them into the average moron who makes up the bulk of the population and the egotistical phonies who think that they are capable of running everything. He despises the lot of them with smug, long-suffering condescension. What is important to him is that he knows his own worth; this is what counts.

The only times he is sick and unable to work are following these mammoth drinking sessions. He cannot understand it, as he goes to sleep in as confident a frame of mind as he has known, only to wake to violent retching, nausea and a feeling that he is crippled. He sweats, shakes, can barely move and is furious with himself. After an hour in the lavatory he dresses himself, gets out of the house unseen and spends the day lying in his truck in a quiet spot. He smokes and sleeps and, by the time dusk falls, he finds that he is beginning to feel better. He decides that, with a little will-power, he might just be able to manage one drink.

Murder

The surviving offspring of these people found dealing with human beings an impossible task. Not difficult; *impossible*. Many people find engaging with other people difficult. Deference, jocularity, get-up-and-go, charisma and the panoply of behaviour, manners, chit-chat and other lubricants of the machinery of relating that are normally drawn upon to negotiate social anxieties do not extend to individuals who have not been raised by human beings. These people are disconnected and disturbed. Their aloofness and peculiar behaviour can lead them to appear intimidating. Disturbed people come in different shapes and sizes, but they share a capacity to say things that are disconcerting, embarrassing and insulting. They may occasionally be insightful, notably where folly is concerned, and they can even be obliging, but on the whole they are not particularly appealing and are prone to being forgotten about.

It is not easy for the average person to imagine what "being forgotten about" might be like, as the idea of existing without other people is extreme and counter-intuitive. Surely contact with people is necessary, especially for a child? Imagine a three or four year-old who gets up in the morning, his father having left and his mother unable to speak to him other than to tell him to get out of her sight. He dresses himself, forages for something to eat, or perhaps doesn't bother, and goes out. There is no-one to meet and nowhere to go, so anything is possible. He may wander the streets, find a garden to play in alone or, if hungry, search for food on the ground, outside a shop or in someone's shopping bag. If it is raining he can sit for hours in a shed or garage watching the weather and playing with dust and pebbles. If the sun is shining, he will probably go to The Woods where he plays his games alone, tentatively trying out an experience of pleasure, but with a worry that he doesn't know what he's doing or why, a worry that shadows every waking moment. When his imagination fails him and there is no-one to offer an alternative idea or different game, he tries to lessen his confusion and ignorance by lying down with his eyes shut, or shouting gobbledegook to himself, or huddling up to a tree to feel embraced. As the day wears on, he tires and his feelings become numb.

Being forgotten about means being forced to live outside the orbit of people, and this engenders bewilderment, constant anxiety and, at times, such a fear that it has to be ignored if he is to stay alive. To succumb to extreme fear with no-one to help would probably end in catastrophe. He is unable to contextualise who he is, where he is or why. Solutions to problems aren't available, comfort is missing and the solitude he turns to, which he finds so relieving, congeals into torpor and an apprehension that something unpleasant is going to happen. He takes care to steer clear of people. He may provoke conflict if he does come into contact with someone. This self-created persecution is not easy to understand, as his primary concern is to remain invisible. As his needs get the better of him—for understanding, food, parental care—and these go unmet hour after hour, daily, weekly, monthly, year upon year, so his anger deepens. The more angry he is the less able he is to feel it or recognise it and the more afraid he becomes that it is other people who are angry with him. He can find himself so petrified by people (his fear of his murderous rage compounded by the imagined hostility) that most of his energy may be expended on fending off contact.

By the time each afternoon or evening arrives he is morose and cut off, drifting past images that no longer hold any symbolic meaning for him. The grass, trees, sky, road, houses and people now seem two-dimensional and vacuous, ogling him as though proclaiming his vulgarity. "Look! Rubbish, dross, tramp!" they seem to chant, mocking him. Estrangement on this scale plays tricks with the senses. The size and shape of objects become distorted: he sees leaves and berries as unusually large, whilst rows of houses wend their way to a horizon that is either cruelly out of reach or else threatens to engulf him. He stares for a long time at a bottle of lemonade in a shop window, unable to comprehend why he cannot pick up something that is inches from his hand. It does not move. It does not move again. He hates it for its independence and defiance. He hears more acutely. His soles scraping the earth trigger a distant landslide; car engines boil with rage; a wasp hums like a foghorn as it seeks a tender spot to stab and twist. He is disorientated as to time, which has lost its meaning. Why should time matter anyway, when each minute, each hour is the same? When waking up is no different from going to sleep? When past, present and future are fused? Reaching the end of a day consumes all that he has, and more.

Losing a sense of space disturbs him more than losing a sense of time. He struggles with how close or far-off objects are. The prospect of reaching the other side of the street sometimes feels unattainable, so distant is it. Clouds stalk and encircle him so that he is forced to sit with his hands covering his head. His legs and feet feel so far away that he can no longer touch them. At these times he is at his most confused and frightened. He can think of nothing further to do to protect himself. He sits quietly rocking, holding himself, clinging to his invisibility, no longer believing that his predators will overlook him.

If experiences like these become routine and persist over years, he can only endure them by inhabiting an extraterrestrial world in which people do not exist, other than as large insects: primitive foes to be avoided. Dealing with them is harrow-

ing and time-consuming, but he at least has time
on his side as very little happens in his world.
Were anyone permitted access to it, they might
imagine that nothing was taking place at all in its
interminable silence and its stagnant, lunar land-
scape, and they would be right. Except, that is, for
the pebble they failed to notice on their arrival.
How could they have noticed it when its form was
indistinguishable from a thousand others? Yet,
didn't it move? It can't have, impossible, but it
did, slowly, imperceptibly into a dark crevice, like
crustacean camouflage that artfully beguiles perception by making the illusion of non-existence
seem real. If our visitor had arrived in the night,
how would he have known that the blackened,
charred trunk of an ancient, broad oak that now
lies outstretched, outlined by moonlight was, during daylight, standing upright, its dead branches
delicately easing the trunk towards slumber?

Within the pebble that went undetected is a
small heart. His task is to ensure that this heart
continues beating, unbeknown to anyone. Nothing
else is of any consequence: not the past, the future
or the lunatic environment outside. Only the moment and the preservation of the life of one un-
known, unchronicled creature. This need to attend
to the present leaves him alert and in a state of
continuous crisis. An intimate, early acquaintance
with death has endowed him with acuity and for-
bearance few children will ever be required to de-
velop. This heightened condition derives from
familiarity with the threat of annihilation but also
yields an unforeseen corollary; infinite patience.

So close has he come to being crushed to death that death is now his closest companion. Everything else is, in comparison, trivial and can be patiently, eternally borne. It goes without saying that there is one experience that remains outside his capability, and this is the capacity to relax. His attempts to relax have served only to make him anxious that he is leaving the pebble unprotected.

Surprisingly, his preoccupation with annihilation no longer has to do with any threat from the external world around him. It may best be thought of as a memory of the fire-branding of his mind as an infant by murder, a memory that is alive in each chromosome, as though taking place currently. This, again, is not easy to think about. How can we conceive of him as feeling continually murdered, day in, day out, and what might it feel like?

One way of thinking about it might be to imagine a frightened, defeated child crouched in the corner of a cold, empty room, crying. Now try to imagine that no words of comfort or offers of help are capable of removing his fear. Not that he does not want it removed. On the contrary, he hates the way he feels but, like multiple sclerosis, diabetes or schizophrenia, his fear has evolved into a chronic illness that has him in its grip. Waking up, eating, looking out of a window, standing still, being spoken to, touching anything, walking, reading—all make him afraid that something terrible will happen. Every moment of each day and night, something fatal feels imminent. This is not possible to imagine, is it, any more than it is to imagine yourself being continually shot or your flesh permanently raw and weeping? Shocking, overwhelming events are meant to happen only once. He knows that this is not so for him. Fear strikes so deep in him—not because of fear itself but because beneath the fear he knows he is helpless to resist anything, especially fear. This helplessness has led to a permanent, life-threatening state of affairs. It is not that he is afraid of people or events or of life, although he is. He is afraid of his response to fear. To feel afraid is, for him, to confront annihilation, irrespective of the scale of the particular fear. All fear feels fatal. For this there is no treatment, no cure and no recovery. Under these circumstances, suicide might seem a reasonable, even civilised option.

His alternative, so far, to suicide is a capacity for infinite patience. He is able to wait. To wait for the rainfall to end, darkness to fall, hunger to abate, morning to break, terror to exhaust him. Do you possess the capacity to wait? We normally associate patience with the ability to place ourselves in another's shoes, to see the situation from their point of view and allow them the time or space they need before it is our turn to have our needs attended to. Do we do this out of love? Expediency? Calculation? Cynicism? Whatever our motive, noble or base, we employ patience in a context of reciprocity. We demonstrate concern and we expect it to be returned. Can you imagine patience with little or no expectation of a return? It doesn't make sense: why would a person wait indefinitely with no prospect of their patience being rewarded?

Only the pebble has the answer to this question. If, at this point in his brief life, the continuing beat of the pebble's heart has become the only thing that matters to him, then by definition nothing else is important. The pebble survived at a time in its history when it was defenceless. It knows that this event was, and forever will be, the greatest achievement of its life. The worst is over. He harbours a thought that he cannot think. Perhaps one day, under different circumstances, in an entirely different world, the pebble may crack in the heat and the creature whose heartbeat he has defended will be allowed to emerge. Meanwhile hostility, humiliation, starvation, isolation, illness, bullying can be managed, to a greater or lesser extent, by waiting. Because nothing can hurt him on the scale it once did, his knowledge that the worst is past gives rise to apparent courage in adversity. However, waiting in these terms needs to be conceived of less as an act of courage or patience and more as a silent expression of resistance. His capacity to wait is a political declaration that he is not prepared to accede entirely to the conditions that have been imposed upon him, and will wait, for as long as is necessary, rather than alter this position, which would be suicidal. He is able to walk the streets daily, speak to no-one, sit through classes without understanding a word, occupy himself until Christmas is over, watch cars go by for weeks and eventually pass an entire school holiday studying an acorn. He waits and waits, not as a means to an end, but as a way of life.

It is not hard to see how this strategy of waiting, no matter how sincere, could lead him into, not only out of, difficulty. He sees waiting as protection, a resistance against impingement and a stance made all the more essential by his private hopes for the pebble. One day, having out-waited all opposition in the world, its turn will come. But he is young and bewildered and does not know that a means to an end and a way of life are not the same thing. To truly resolve his confusion he would need to consider three further things, which, of course, he is unable to do: first, the relationship between waiting and his strategy of becoming invisible to his mother; second, his fear of his fear and third; his First and Second Principles.

Could his resolve to wait be a way of modifying his invisibility by altering it to a level of semitransparency, because constant invisibility is unbearable? It is a reasonable speculation. If so, the risk of waiting might be that he finds himself in a half-way house between invisibility and nakedness. To dread annihilation as a result of fear is no simple succession of feelings. Why does he feel as though his skin has been torn off and he is defenceless? Waking up, eating, looking out of a window, reading a book, standing still, being spoken to—none of these activities is in itself terrifying, so what is it that gets into him? Could he be so punch drunk as to experience any life event as a threat of death? Why a death threat, which implies murderous violence? We have learned that he was threatened with murder and that, given the murder of Carole, his assessment of the situation needs to be taken seriously. To complicate matters further, he has revealed how he sees himself as violent. Of the Five Principles he devised to stay alive, one is more closely related than the others to his lifelong terror of being killed. His Second Principle, *Anger will keep me alive*, afforded him a glimpse of outrage that he could not allow himself to feel openly, but which he knew was appropriate under the circumstances. If an attempt is made on your life and you are not exhausted and close to defeat, outrage and anger are sane, self-preservative responses. Is it possible that the branding into his memory of murder and attempted murder is made intolerable by the added wish to murder those responsible for what happened to Carole, Patricia and him? In an exposed state, as the pebble was, acting on murderous impulses would have been suicidal, not to mention unmanageable. Reprisal had to remain the stuff of fantasy, not reality. These were not fantasies that could be shared with parents who might understand and allay them. By opening his mouth the risk of being savaged further, maybe killed, would have increased.

Harbouring angry feelings that you can never speak about can drive you mad. Emotions coagulate in the resulting confusion, especially in children, which is why talking about them is essential. If this cannot happen, knowing where someone else's feelings end and yours begin is difficult, even impossible, to figure out. The power of fantasy can lead to victimisation, scapegoating, bullying and cold-hearted cruelty, sometimes with barely a word having been spoken. In his case, a vicious circle was set up between memories of savagery and the corresponding rage at having had to endure it. To save his sanity, he could not abandon his anger, but holding onto anger that has no outlet jeopardises the sanity he depends on.

To deal with a seemingly insoluble conflict, he held onto the *idea* of his anger, whilst disowning the feelings that risked laying him low. In other words, his mind banished the pain and turmoil of fury, sadistic pleasure, anxiety and guilt, all of which ensued from his rage, whilst retaining a kernel of knowledge about why he was angry in the first place, in the belief that this would keep him sane. This may be fine in theory, but far less so in practice. Unable to feel, he became vulnerable to imagining that people were angry with him when they were not. We have all met people who are like this. Anyone who has been cornered by someone yelling "What are you looking at?" will know how easy it is for someone to get the wrong end of the stick. Milder versions of it happen every day. If, at 9.30pm during a dinner party, a guest says "I would like to go home now" you can be fairly sure that someone, perhaps you, will take offence at what is an otherwise innocuous announcement. In mental hospitals, some patients are convinced that the nurse or doctor is out to kill them: doubts and conflicts have been done away with altogether. Our minds play tricks on us. One of the most confusing is to attribute to other people feelings that we can't tolerate in ourselves. Used in moderation this might occasionally be useful but if it becomes a habit, as it did with him, it skews our grip on reality. His mind crumpled under the combined impact of memories of violence and the disavowed rage they stirred up in him.

This millstone of internalised violence that gave rise to this vicious circle, oppressive as it is, he believes is not the fundamental reason why he is terrified of fear. In his view, the problem devolves to the First Principle: *Everything I say and do is wrong.* Of all the Principles, with the exception of the Fifth, this defines most accurately who he is. It is more reliable than DNA testing and, like his constitution, structures him and his view of the world. A qualification is needed lest this idea seems sweeping and over-inclusive. Imagine you are *wrong*. Being wrong defines you prior to and including any psychological or physical trait. It does *not* mean you are a person who has the capacity to be right but who has made the mistake of doing something wrong and needs correcting. Nothing you do can ever be right, because right is an anomalous category insofar as it pertains to you. Each thought, feeling, perception, physical action, encounter, dream, wish or memory is wrong *a priori*, without you having comparative knowledge of what "right" might mean. You are only and always wrong, in the way you might be Afro-Caribbean, Caucasian or female. You are wrong because you should not be here. You should not exist. An appalling mistake was made when you shamelessly proffered yourself to those who now pay the price for your vulgar importuning.

Life under these circumstances is not viable. The unrelenting message you feed yourself, every moment, is: "You are wrong." It is tempting and reasonable to feel concerned about the corrosive effect of this on a young mind, or to ask what could be done to salvage the self-esteem of someone so mentally incarcerated. He would caution you to conserve your energy, as you would be addressing a problem that does not exist. There is no-one to protect and no self-esteem to save. These are pastimes for the living, luxuries for a day when, as an adult, the concept of having needs he is entitled to might enter his mind for the first time. At this point he may beseech you, without much hope of success, to master the fact that the person you mistake him for has not yet been invented, other than by you.

He knows why he is afraid of his fear. He barely survives on what he can scavenge and is operating at the limits of his abilities. If he lets loose the rage that permeates him it would put himself at further risk of going the way of Carole. At least he is alive and can take steps to stay this way. What he can never quantify or control is how and when his constant rage might tilt the balance between his need to scrape together the daily resources he needs to survive and the consequence of losing any of them. Think about how this fear might frighten him. Not fear of death—this is *our* fear. Think of what it would mean to orchestrate knowingly a situation in which he places himself at risk of death, given all he has learned about his insane situation. The ignominy would not be death, but that he would have been personally re-sponsible—no-one else—for his own demise. He would not even have the dubious justification of suicide to partially redeem him. The colossal error would be to invoke his own annihilation under the delusional belief that standing up for himself might change his parents. There is no evidence to suggest that this is even remotely possible. To go against his experience would be dishonesty and complete madness. The consequence of his failure would be to perversely unite him with his parents through compelling proof that what he says and does *is* wrong: conclusive evidence that they were right all along.

Yet not even this is the worst of it. The last, un-speakable act would be the most shameful of all. He would have repeated, of his own volition, his parents' barbarity towards their offspring. He would have forsaken the pebble.

THE FIFTH PRINCIPLE

I could not live by myself or die by my own hand. I drifted without purpose, trying to stay alive whilst avoiding people. By the age of six, I had floated to the margins of groups, gatherings, classes, conversations, meetings or any setting where people got together. If they milled around I melted into the shadows. If they crossed my path, I yielded. If they pushed me out of the way (on a pavement, in a queue, at a shop) I gave up and walked off, even if searching for food. Nothing was worth the bother. If I was obliged to speak, it would be through a cliché or something so tangential (such as a diversionary lie) that talk ground to a halt. The exception to these rules of silence and keeping my distance was the period of startling outbreaks of chatter in the school classroom.

This is not strictly true. There was one further breach of the rule to stay quiet and avoid people, for which I paid a price, and this occurred during a breaktime one day at primary school. I was sitting in the schoolyard when I saw the teacher, Mister Adamson, walk over to a boy from my class, Michael Broadey, and put his arm around his shoulder. Together, they strolled off across the playing field and seemed to be deep in conversation. I could not resist following them, even though I knew I shouldn't. Although I was trying to catch what they were saying, I think the reason I could not help but follow them was because I was overcome by a need to feel included. I could just overhear Adamson explaining the offside rule to Michael, who was a keen footballer, and crept up a little closer. Too close, as it turned out. Adamson caught sight of me out of the corner of his eye, whirled round, his black teacher's gown billowing in the breeze, and roared: "I AM NOT TALK- ING TO *YOU!*"

I jumped. His anger shocked me but this on its own was not what upset me, as by then I had become used to it. What mortified me was seeing Michael smiling and the children in the playground pointing and laughing. I wanted the ground to open up. I slunk away, vowing never to speak to Adamson again, a resolution I kept.

I had some awareness that I tended to feel out of control when I came into contact with other people, so I made increasing efforts to avoid them and was vigilant about lapses. In my growing isolation I misread kindness for falseness, confidence for arrogance and love for sentimental manipulation. These distortions of perception led to the progressive skewing of reality described earlier. At the outset it had been necessary to hold onto my sanity by tearing myself away from my mother and the instinct to depend upon her. I knew that this counter-intuitive strategy was critical if I was to avoid succumbing to her madness and being destroyed. However, in the absence of parenting and under the pressure of her constant attacks, the avoidance of human contact established itself as an appropriate, normal course of action in my mind, and eventually became an end in itself.

Having not known what parenting was, the loneliness I experienced did not affect me in the way it might another person. It was preferable to what had gone before. I did not make the connection between loneliness and needing people. Solitude brought safety and relief, and I wanted as much of this as possible, so loneliness seemed a small price to pay. I never moved incrementally from loneliness to painful isolation to despair. For me, it was the experience of people that produced isolation and despair, not the lack of it. Only at a certain point, far down the line, when prolonged invisibility tipped into the threat of disappearance and annihilation, did solitude switch to terror and a frantic need to eat would grip me. Even then, I had little thought of turning to people to get help.

For the most part, I was an unnoticed figure who spent the years of childhood alone learning little, if anything, about life, people or relationships. I had tried to assimilate two lessons. I was not wanted, and needed to become invisible if I was to avoid dying or being driven mad. Although assaulted and tormented by problems that were too complex for any child to deal with, out-

wardly my life appeared simple. I did nothing.
The streets, The Woods, time, space, even the
weather coalesced into one unbroken experience
of drifting interminably. I sleepwalked through
grey days, neither looking backward nor forward,
my mind attending to basic survival needs and the
management of time that barely moved. This life-
less vacuum echoed the emptiness of the house in
which I lived; a boarding house in which people
slept but otherwise were barely aware of each other. Mealtimes, evenings, weekends did not exist
and other markers of passing time such as the seasons, festivities and birthdays were ignored. The
scale of deprivation was not due primarily to eco-
nomic poverty. We were poor working class, but
so were other families in our street who seemed to
be happier and more involved with each other. My
parents hated other people, so that living together,
being a family, was torture.

The lack of stimulation in childhood was punc-
tuated by outbursts of capricious violence that
were a feature of my mother's psychotic personality and my parents' disastrous relationship. Emptiness and numbness were the backcloth to my and
my sister's experience of violence, but this brought
no relief or peace. We were conditioned, in our retreat into silence, to expect attack whenever we
were in the house. As a result, I found myself living in two contradictory states of mind. One was a
persistent need to get food whilst avoiding being
savaged, and the other was an unrequited craving
to find respite from these threats of violence and
pressures to survive. The effect of living in these

two states of mind was like being incessantly short-circuited. Electricity was being pumped into me but could find no outlet. My body was innervated yet disconnected from people and the world around me. I could not rest, sleep or relax; neither could I think, talk or act. I was paralysed, trapped between two colossal magnets pulling me in different directions.

A narrow, arid existence characterised by blank expanses of concrete and infinite silence defeated what hope I had. My blunted personality stumbled on, ignorant of pleasure or being cared for. From the time I went to school the attacks by my mother were supplemented by my father's derision. His accusation was that everything I did, said or thought was fake—I was a counterfeit person. There are people in the world who are false. We have probably all met them. One characteristic of such people is that they seem to be unaware of the falseness of their behaviour, even though it is apparent to us, and this is one reason why it is uncomfortable to be with them. It is as though they are covering up something but not doing a good job of it, except to themselves. I may have behaved falsely, but it was not on the basis of needing to cover up something bad. I knew I *was* bad. And fake. I had believed my mother and father. There was, to my eternal shame, nothing real about me. When I did find myself behaving slightly more normally (for example, when I was away from my parents) I experienced my behaviour as false, and this is what I covered up, as it contrasted so markedly with what I knew to be the truth—that I was fake.

During these early years my body as well as my mind deteriorated—malnutrition, rotten teeth, asthma, scarring due to cuts, misshapen feet jammed into small shoes, faecal incontinence, lice, etc. Mercifully, I did not notice the impact of these things until later. Conscious knowledge of my Principles seemed to fade as I became preoccupied with a hand to mouth existence. One vestige of the Principles did persist, however, in the form of a recurrent thought. I was not able to rid myself of one version or other of the idea *"I must leave as soon as I get a chance"*. It played on my mind, I realise, like a far-flung refrain from some guardian angel I did not recognize. The thought that one day I might get away did not leave me and settled into me not so much as a practical plan, but as a vision or goal towards which I strove. This gave me the will to go on. I understand with hindsight that this thought was connected to my Third Prin! ciple—*Anger will keep me alive*—and that the Principles had not died completely. I view it as remarkable that such a thought could have stayed alive in me. How it happened I did not know, until the meaning of the miracle of the Resurrection of Carole, and the unpredictable benefits it brought me, became clearer. Another component was the hope I felt when I saw beauty. I had melted when I saw the Alfa Romeo, or the thrilling dusk of The Woods or families in cars.

The next and final step in this story requires a leap of the imagination across many years, keeping in mind, if possible, the link to the childhood vow to get away from my circumstances as soon as I got a chance. It means telescoping the decades between childhood and middle age. Before we make the leap, I want to mention two persistent regrets that have stayed with me through my life as a consequence of the things I have recounted. One is completely irrational, but no less powerful for that, and the other is more rational, although probably still irrational. I regret never having been able to do anything to keep Carole alive. I know this is and was impossible, as she died before I was born, but hardly a day has gone by when I have not thought of this suffering child and how, if only I had been able to help get her the care and attention she needed—which was not great—she might have lived. I know that this is unrealistic and I can live with the reality that nothing could have been done. The remorse does not drive me to distraction. It is a regret that flows from a particular vale of tears the source of which I cannot forsake, no matter how much I have tried.

The second regret is that I did not do more to help my sister, Patricia. This is, in some ways, a more serious matter as I was alive during Patricia's childhood and should have been able to do more, as my parents all but destroyed her. Again, I have learned not to torment myself with self-recrimination. I understand more than I did about why I could not help her. I was a child at the limit of my capacity to survive, with nothing to offer. For all I know I might have been jealous of the arrival of another mouth to feed when I was starving. I feel sorry for the arrogance and contempt I at times felt and displayed towards Patricia, which she at no time deserved.

Like every child, I had taken my model of how to be a person from those who were meant to care for me. It was inevitable that, despite my instinctive response to my mother's behaviour as inhuman and wrong, and my determination to differentiate myself from her and her destructiveness, I should, nevertheless and despite myself, reproduce many of her ideas and attitudes. It is not always, if ever, easy to see when this happens. The disowning of unpleasant knowledge about oneself can take place on such an efficient, far-reaching scale that the merest hint from anyone that I might in any way be like my mother could well have been met with contempt or derision, probably of a variety not dissimilar from my mother's or father's. Reclaiming and owning these truths at times felt as difficult as some of the darkest experiences Patricia and I endured as children.

I have no illusion that what happened to me can be erased or "cured". Neither the situation nor the people responsible could have been changed, despite my delusional belief that this was possible. The only aspect of the situation that could change was me. Through this knowledge, I was able, in adulthood and with careful help, to forge a Fifth Principle that permitted me to live without denying the reality of the past but also without being shackled to it or constrained by the million conscious and unconscious tentacles that sway, confuse, judge and inveigle us into dwelling within received opinion. The Fifth Principle, when I first came across it, out of the blue, in the context of the work I was doing on what had happened to me, seemed ridiculous, outrageous, dangerous and irresponsible. It took months before I could begin to consider taking it seriously and address the important truth that underlay it. Its accuracy was startling, despite it seeming superficially crass and devastatingly obvious. Perhaps I had never been in a position to think this way before. Perhaps everything I had done to address the past had prepared me for the discovery, but this did not take away the shock of realising what I needed to do.

During my early adult life, I had invested every last ounce of energy in undoing the damage of my childhood, yet the effects lingered. The difficulty in saying no, a chronic tendency to withdraw and to overwork, self-critical beliefs about my appearance and worth and above all, a legacy of shame that I had never found lasting ways to diminish. I had concluded that these were inevitable consequences of awful luck and that I should bear them with fortitude whilst making the most of what I had, which was a great deal compared to my childhood. The difficulty was that this didn't work. I knew I was not happy, but at the same time I wasn't confident enough to tackle head-on the distress that lay within me. With some skilled, unflinching help, I looked square in the face each thought, feeling and idea that impaired me. It wasn't easy and soon I discovered a reservoir of shame and rage that I never thought could run so deep.

I dived in.

Out of this no-holds-barred examination, which took time, emerged a realisation that I needed to remain faithful to the logic of my early Principles, which were probably the sanest things I had ever thought. The First Principle was my definition of the nature of the problem I had faced—everything I said or did was, I felt, wrong. The subsequent three Principles were strategies for survival in insane circumstances. The final Fifth Principle turned out to be a next logical step in the formulation of the sequence of Principles. It took the form of a renunciation of the previous four Principles, the conditions under which they were formulated and the circumstances in which Carole, Patricia and I had been required to exist. The truth was that there had never been any hope of improving my childhood situation. I needed to understand once and for all that my circumstances had been irredeemable and that no amount of effort to salvage, repair or improve them would make, or have made, the slightest difference. To imagine otherwise was an illusion out of which grew the delusional wish I had maintained as a child that I could change my mother. It was necessary to reject the very premises, as well as the attitudes and conduct, of my upbringing. By remaining preoccupied with it, angry with it, concerned about it, sad about it, I was draining myself of what energy I had left that might otherwise go into living. Formulating the Fifth Principle was not a denial of the past, an act of pique or an attempt to triumph over my parents. On the contrary, it represented an extension by an adult mind of a childhood realisation. I had been born into a concentration camp and as soon as I had the opportunity, I should leave. The Fifth Principle itself could not have been specified or implemented by a child. As a boy, I had been dependent on my surroundings for survival and could not risk what little I had by throwing these over. It was only in adulthood, with a certain amount of independence, that I felt strong enough to deal with my final, remaining ties to a nihilistic world of depravity and hatred. Putting the Fifth Principle into words was not easy, as not only did it need to come from adult thinking, it needed to remain faithful to its inspiration which was the desire to get away, miraculously lodged in my mind since childhood, and which enabled me to leave home for France—and forever—at seventeen. After much reflection backwards and forwards across the decades, a phrase mysteriously announced itself, uninvited, that captured the essence of what I wanted to communicate. I could not accept it, yet no matter which way I analysed it, it worked at every level and stubbornly refused to leave my mind. My Fifth Principle became: *Fuck It*.

Through this Principle I finally began to overturn the legacy of shame and terror from my childhood by dismantling, piece by piece, the premises upon which patterns of thinking and feeling from the past controlled me. I now realised, after a long time, that it might be possible to become able to do what I wanted to do: love, cry in public, be angry, ignore other people's madness, listen to music and, to my surprise, write, if I were to become able to persistently and deeply renounce the state of affairs under which I was born and grew up, and their legacy in my own thinking. I had finally got it; no amount of adaptation, repair or improvement would deliver the internal freedom I needed in order to feel alive. The entire, murderous arrangement that had been indefensible from the start, had to go. *Fuck It*.

The power of *Fuck It* lay not merely in the renunciation of past premises that I have emphasised so far, but in the dismantling of forms of attachment to these premises *in the present*. By immersing myself deeply in the past and allowing its significance and meaning to touch every part of me, I became able to free myself of its hold over me. Being required to remain preoccupied by insoluble problems associated with surviving or not surviving was a straitjacket, and this was gradually discarded. Eventually, I began to understand that I could do what *I* wanted to do, something I had thought I believed, but which I had not put into practice. I had put others first and had been proud of the fact, at great cost to me. I came to understand that I did not have to overwork. I did not have to work hard, if I didn't want to. I did not have to attend meetings if I didn't want to, go to dinner parties, answer questions or even talk. Neither did I have to withdraw, be inert or remain silent, if I didn't want to. What startled me was that none of this was destructive. Before the emergence of the Fifth Principle I would probably have judged these attitudes as egotistical, uncharitable and immature. The truth was that I rarely put my needs or wishes first. I had created a virtue out of self-effacement and overwork, beneath which dwelt resentment and despair. Fuck It.

Living by the Fifth Principle took some getting used to. Two guiding ideas helped. First and most importantly, I realised that I had nothing to lose compared to what had been at stake as a child. Second, the acceptance that I, like everyone, was going to die (not suicidally, self-destructively or prematurely, but naturally—I was in the second half of life) was an effective counterbalance to fears of loss. My anxieties about the opprobrium of others who might not approve of the *Fuck It* philosophy dissipated. I could now reclaim unequivocally my integrity and be honest with others without excessive fear. Fuck It. Why not?

It is not straightforward to imagine renunciation of this kind, as the usual use of *Fuck It* denotes an attack on the power of an other and an attempt to reverse who is powerful and who is helpless. What it also denotes is that the terms of the engagement between the powerful and the helpless remain unchanged. I had no use for this kind of peripheral change. My definition of *Fuck It* involved something different: a rejection of the underlying *terms* upon which the insane logic of my upbringing was based, and the institution of a fundamentally new set of terms unaffected by the use or misuse of power. Once these new terms were in place it became impossible to revert to engagement with others on the basis of who is powerful and who is helpless.

An unusual discovery was that the *Fuck It* philosophy needed to be found and re-found, many times, before it settled into a philosophy of my own. Even then, re-finding it to deal with instances of oppression was indispensable, as each situation was different and demanded its own response. What united these responses was the different terms on which they were now based.

A particular, unexpected consequence of adopting the Fifth Principle was that I became more able to show those I valued that I loved them. I can't speak for others, but if you have one or two people you love and can talk to, I think you're lucky. As for everyone else, they can be set into perspective according to their priority instead of assuming unrealistic importance. In the past, they would have become confused with powerful internal figures and phantasms, resulting in my feeling as if I were—and sometimes actually becoming—controlled by their influence. Well, Fuck It. They can do what they like.

Living according to the Fifth Principle made it possible for me to evolve from a disturbed person into a strange person. By strange, I am referring to those individuals who are not conventional in that they struggle with difficult and complex feelings, without rejecting any of them in favour of a charade of normality, no matter how seemingly intelligent or sophisticated. I hope that more strange people venture into the world. Strange people are interesting and there are not enough of them. As far as I am concerned, the more the better.

Slowly, I have come to feel proud of being a strange person. That, as they say, is another story.

APPENDIX

The Five Principles:

1. Everything I say and do is wrong.

2. I do not believe what I am told. The truth is the opposite of what I am told.

3. Anger will keep me alive.

4. If I work twice as hard as anyone else, I might be able to live a life that approximates to a normal life.

5. Fuck it.